SAINT NICK 2

BRADLEY WRIGHT

ALSO BY BRADLEY WRIGHT

Alexander King

THE SECRET WEAPON

COLD WAR

MOST WANTED

Alexander King Prequels

WHISKEY & ROSES

VANQUISH

KING'S RANSOM

KING'S REIGN

SCOURGE

Lawson Raines

WHEN THE MAN COMES AROUND

SHOOTING STAR

Saint Nick

SAINT NICK

SAINT NICK 2

Saint Nick 2

Copyright © 2020 by **Bradley Wright**
All rights reserved. No part of this publication may be reproduced, distributed or transmitted in any form or by any means, without prior written permission.
Bradley Wright/King's Ransom Publishing
www.bradleywrightauthor.com
Publisher's Note: This is a work of fiction. Names, characters, places, and incidents are a product of the author's imagination. Locales and public names are sometimes used for atmospheric purposes. Any resemblance to actual people, living or dead, or to businesses, companies, events, institutions, or locales is completely coincidental.
Saint Nick 2/ Bradley Wright. -- 1st ed.
ISBN - 9798575455363

"Let's be naughty and save Santa the trip."

— Gary Allan

"The main reason Santa is so jolly is because he knows where all the bad girls live."

— George Carlin

Saint Nick 2

1

The snow had just begun to trickle from the darkening sky just outside of Nick Campos's office. The new office he'd had built away from all the workshops. Away from his eager little elf, Zeke, and his never-ending ideas for the latest technology that Nick could use when he suited up as Santa—*Savior of the Universe!*—as Zeke would always say. And he even liked the more secluded location of his daily workplace because it was away from home. It wasn't that he didn't enjoy being around Brooke either, actually, quite the opposite. He'd never been more in love in his entire life. However, sometimes, a man just needs to be alone with his thoughts. And as he poured another couple fingers of George T. Stagg Kentucky bourbon into his glass, sometimes a man just needed to be alone with his whiskey.

"That's an awfully good bottle of bourbon there Mr. Campos. Don't you think you should be sharing it with someone special?"

Nick turned to find Brooke standing in the doorway, leaning back against the wood trim.

"I think I'd love to, Mrs. Campos."

She was stunning in her wedding dress. Her natural blonde hair was pinned up for the occasion, drawing attention to the sharp lines on her thin face. Nick loosened the bow-tie around his neck. It was the first time he'd ever worn one. It would also be his last. Though he wasn't fond of it, he wasn't wearing it for himself, he was wearing it for his new bride. He grabbed another glass from his bar cart and poured one for his girl. She walked over and unbuttoned the collar on his shirt, and gave him a long kiss.

"I'm sorry I slipped away for a minute," Nick said. "Everyone is out there celebrating our day but me. It's just, you know—"

"I know how you get when you know something terrible is happening and you think you can stop it," Brooke finished for him. "It's okay that you can't fix everything all the time. It's okay to dance at your wedding even though others are suffering. It doesn't make you a bad man, Nick. Would I have married you if you were?"

"I'm not sure why you married me," Nick said with a devilish grin. "Except for my dashing good looks, my razor sharp wit, and my ways in the bedroom."

"Oh of course," Brooke laughed and rolled her eyes. "But mostly you know I love you for your humility."

They clinked glasses and shared a sip. There were a lot of things that turned Nick on about his wife, but the fact that she could share a bourbon neat with him was right up there at the top.

"Listen," she said. "This stuff will be here tomorrow. You can relax and enjoy one night off. Let's go have a good time. We're ready to cut the cake . . ."

Nick smiled. "You know I don't eat cake." Nick patted his six pack. He never took days off of the diet either. And he certainly could not afford to take the night off from work. Because evil sure as hell didn't. The All Seeing Eye was a fantastic piece of technology. The ability to see what anyone was doing at any time was priceless in the world of fighting the bad guys. However, when a man can study it every day, all day, and *always* see someone doing wrong, he forever feels guilty when he isn't doing something about it.

Even on his wedding day.

"I know. And I know how important this is to you," she nodded toward the ASE. "I'm always fighting right there with you. But don't you think I deserve you for one night?"

Nick felt terrible. He knew it wasn't fair to her the way he obsessed over things. But it had been particularly bad lately. Human trafficking was at an all time high, and if Santa Claus himself wasn't willing to drop everything to help keep innocent children safe, then who the hell would be?

There was a knock at the door. Allen Despaw, Nick's oldest friend in the world walked in. He was a big man—6' 3" inches and 275 pounds of solid muscle. He had a long biker beard and a permanent hell-raising-grin on his face. Allen had been staying at the North Pole the last couple of months. Nick needed help with his evil fighting operation, and there was no better qualified man than his Special Forces vet and best friend. It was damn good to have a normal guy in town to watch football and smoke cigars with as well. But right now, Nick knew that Allen was going to give him hell for being in the war room on his wedding night. And Nick supposed he deserved it.

"What the hell are you doing in here, you two? You'll have all the privacy you want in a couple hours. Right now it's time to party!"

Brooke looked over at Nick and melted him with a smile. A man as lucky as he was should never let his woman think she's not appreciated. Even though the evil he was about to go after was as bad as it gets in the world, he at the very least owed her this.

"Let's party then," Nick said.

"Hell yeah!" Allen raised his glass.

Brooke took Nick by the hand and led him down the hall. Allen ran ahead to give the MC a heads up so he could announce their entry. Brooke paused at the door and turned into him. She placed her hand on his cheek and caressed the stubble he'd refused to shave.

"I love you, Nick. I've never met a man as dedicated to serving others as you. It's one of the reasons I married you. Just give me this night, then I will help you take down every nasty son of a bitch that comes up on your radar tomorrow. Okay?"

Nick smiled, wrapped his arms around her bottom and hoisted her up. "I'm the luckiest man in the world."

"Damn right you are."

They kissed.

"Ladies and gentlemen, let's hear it for your bride and groom, Nick and Brooke Campos!"

The auditorium erupted with shouts and applause. Everyone in the North Pole was there, along with friends and family from the States. Nick let Brooke down and they walked in side by side. Both grinning ear to ear. Though this wasn't Nick's kind of scene at all, he was going to forget himself for at least a couple of hours and enjoy his wife.

As they made their way to the dance floor the deejay started the music. What he played was a surprise to Nick because Brooke had vetoed it from the very beginning. "The Whipping Post" by the Allman Brothers Band blared through the speakers, and his soul caught fire. When he'd suggested it weeks ago, he'd meant it to be sarcastic, and he thought it would be funny, but she hadn't let on for a second. She was definitely the one. And if her playing his favorite song wasn't enough, the bourbon bar in the back of the room that had just caught his eye sealed the deal. She was his forever. The Kentucky boy in him couldn't have been happier. Brooke looked back as he spun her and mouthed "surprise!" through a wide smile. His buddy, Allen, was playing air guitar off to their left. It was a perfect day.

He was happy to get at least one good day in the books that felt like a little piece of heaven. Mostly because he knew what he was about to go through—attempting to take down one of the largest child trafficking rings in the world—was going to be nothing but hell.

2

Nick finished getting dressed after a nice hot shower. Yesterday was one of the greatest days of his life. After all the booze and Brooke keeping him up for hours after they'd made it back home, he was moving a little slow. He wasn't nineteen anymore. Hangovers were a much tougher adversary at forty-one than they used to be. But like always when he was feeling sluggish, he got up and poured himself into a workout. Nothing cleared the cobwebs like busting your ass for an hour and sweating out all the weakness. It was like coffee times ten. Especially when the Jiu Jitsu portion of the routine was with a 275 pound bear like his buddy Allen. Nick was exhausted, but couldn't have been more ready for the day.

Nick walked into the war room and his little workhorse, Zeke, was already pounding away at the keyboard. There were eight flat panel monitors stacked in two rows of four. Before Zeke had left the dance floor last night, Nick had nudged him and told him to do a keyword search today on the All Seeing Eye. Nick had left a list of search words for him. That was what he'd slipped away after the ceremony to do.

The list consisted of words that might in any way, shape, or form be consistent with those that a group of scumbags who are trafficking kids might use. Things like tie them up, sell her, sell him, how much for her or him, and so on. Then the ASE would work its magic that Nick still didn't fully understand, but could make it work. Using all available radio, gamma, and ultraviolet rays, the machine could pick up sights and sounds from anywhere on earth. It worked better if you knew the name and location of the person you were trying to catch, but catching criminals didn't exactly work that way. So like searching Google, the ASE would listen for the search words you typed in all across the globe. It was nothing short of miraculous. And Nick had figured that his little buddy Zeke had probably been at it most of the night. He might be a crazy little son of a bitch, but Zeke was dedicated. Nick could relate to that.

The other thing that Nick had Zeke do was key in on a particular area. It made things a lot easier for the ASE, and for Nick to find who was at the head when they focused in on hotbeds. That was about the only positive in getting help from the CIA. They were mostly a huge pain in Nick's ass, but they did have a lot of good people that he could use for resources like where the most popular places these heinous crimes were occurring. California, Texas, and other most populated places obviously had more cases, but when Nick heard that Atlanta, Georgia was one of the worst cities per capita for trafficking, for some reason he honed in. He wasn't sure if it was because he'd spent some time there when he was younger, or what it was, but that's where he had Zeke focus.

"What do we got, Z?"

Zeke nearly jumped out of his seat. He spun in his chair and stared up at Nick. He wasn't more than three feet tall, pretty typical of the elves at the North Pole. He had an oversized nose, a bushy beard with bushy eyebrows to match. He'd lost about ten pounds since he started doing some workouts with Nick, and for an elf that only weighed a hundred and thirty pounds, he was a lean machine now.

"I got—" Zeke started, then stopped to take a drink of water. The look he was wearing wasn't something Nick was used to seeing. Instead of eagerness, Zeke was giving the vibe that he was sick.

"You okay?"

Zeke finished his water. "I don't like this assignment, boss."

"You think I do?"

"No."

"And that's exactly why we're doing it," Nick said. "Because short of blowing people up like most of the guys we go after are doing, trafficking young kids might be the worst thing someone can do."

Zeke nodded and pick up his notebook. "I've heard more than I ever wanted to hear. I had no idea this was happening so much."

"Then let's do something before it gets any worse."

"There was keyword chatter all around Atlanta," Zeke said. "But specifically in the higher concentrations of homelessness. Even more specifically, some rich guy's home in Buckhead on the North end of the city."

"You're shittin' me. In some ritzy area?" Nick said.

"It gets worse. When I looked up who lived there, I didn't recognize the name until I Googled how he made his money."

"And?"

"His name is Kevin Swayne."

"Shut the hell up," Nick said. He couldn't believe what came out of Zeke's mouth. "*The* Kevin Swayne? Of half the most popular movies in Hollywood history?"

"So you know him?"

"Z my man, unless you live at the North Pole, or under a rock, *everyone* knows Kevin Swayne. He's like an American icon. I never liked the son of a bitch, but most of the world does. There must be some sort of mistake."

Nick would have asked for a replay of what was said, but the ASE still had no way to go back in time, or to record it. Something about the way the waves are used to make an image and produce sounds, still wasn't recordable. Zeke had been working on it for over a year but still hadn't found a way.

"You want to see?" Zeke said.

"What? You figured out how to record on the ASE?"

"Well, sort of." Zeke hopped off his chair and walked over to a desk behind Nick. He pointed to a small camera that was sitting there. "I put a Nest camera here. It runs all the time. I zoomed it in on the screen I was watching your actor there on. It's an analog way to record something, but it works."

"I feel like that was a solution I should have come up with."

"Yeah, would have been more your speed," Zeke said looking up at Nick. "You want to see it?"

"Can you give me the short version? I've got a meeting with the CIA."

"Basically it was a couple minute call about having vans pick up homeless girls. 'The cute ones', was his exact words. Sickening really. They're doing some sort of sweep because there are some rich people in Mexico that want some slave labor. He actually said they are having trouble keeping up with demand. Can you believe that?"

Nick just shook his head.

"Anyway, that's all I could get out of it."

"You mean they didn't say a time and place?"

"He said usual place, usual time."

"Damn." Nick put his hands on his hips. "Try to figure out who was on the—"

"Other end of that call," Zeke interrupted. "Already on it."

"Nice work Z. Let me know something as soon as you have it."

"You got it, boss."

Nick walked out of the war room in disbelief. He had to find out where that meeting was going down and save those kids. And maybe going old school and having an in-person visit with Mr. Hollywood—Kevin Swayne—was the only way to do it.

3

Nick walked out into the darkness. Pitch black outside at noon had taken a long time to get used to. The first couple months he'd spent in the North Pole in the winter his body didn't know when to sleep. It had been the same problem for Brooke. There was a gentle snow falling beneath the streetlights as he walked to the barn. He still hadn't gotten used to the cold either. And he never would. That was one of the many things at the NP —his now forever home—that he couldn't change. It's just the way it was. The elves tried to tell him the Christmas songs that played over a loud speaker all year long, nonstop, were also something he couldn't change, but that had been the first time he'd pulled rank as the new Santa. He had to explain to them that if one more day passed, full of jolly songs, he was going to go Here's Johnny on them, and kill them all.

They stopped their protests immediately.

Nick pressed the button on his key fob that raised the airplane hangar-like door on the front of the barn. "Barn" was a relative term at that point. Out of the many changes

Nick had made to the NP village, the barn was maybe the biggest. When he'd first arrived, it had actually been a barn that housed the most famous reindeer on the planet. Now, he'd added an entire hangar to the front of it that stored some of his winter toys, along with some of Zeke's more elaborate special creations.

As the hangar door rose, special heaters kicked on that blew hard enough to keep the subzero temperatures out. When the door was high enough, Nick saw one of his favorite implementations that would never make it to the Santa stories they tell the kids. His brand new Santa *sleigh*. And to him, it was a beauty. A completely reconfigured military alpha Humvee. Full of some of Zeke's finest technological and weaponry upgrades. And of course, painted cherry red, in an ode to the fat man himself.

The elves hated it. And so did old Mrs. Claus. They claimed it made a mockery of Santa's tradition. Nick didn't care. He was the one that had to ride in it, and from the moment he first rode in the original sleigh, he couldn't fathom how riding in an open cockpit high in the sky, whether it was cold or not, ever made any sense to Santa, or anyone else. Sure, his first trip into the North Pole when Santa had passed along his powers was magical. But even with the heaters blowing on him in that original sleigh, it was freezing.

Not only were the black leather heated seats in his new Humvee sleigh more comfortable, he had cupholders and a built-in screen to watch tv if he had to wait somewhere. It was a no-brainer. Not to mention, sometimes when the reindeer flew him somewhere, he wanted to be like a normal civilian again, with the ability to unhook from the reindeer and just drive around. The elves and Mrs. Claus didn't understand any of that, because they'd always lived there at the North Pole. But sometimes flying down to the beach, unhooking, rolling down your windows and cranking some "Free Bird" by Skynard was the highlight of his week. And when Brooke would go with him, they could actually pull up to a restaurant and have a normal dinner. In short, he thought it was brilliant. And there was still plenty of room for guests, and his Santa sack when it was needed.

Nick stepped inside the hangar. A couple of elves were hooking up the reindeer to the front of the Humvee sleigh. He watched as Jack came over to greet him and give him whatever pertinent information he might need about where he was going. If Zeke was the crazy genius elf who concocted and built all the technology and toys for Nick, Jack was the gruff little guy that was always all business, and kept Nick focused on the task at hand. Though Zeke was more Nick's style, he needed Jack all the same. It kept Nick from doing the legwork on all the missions they'd been working.

"Director Crawford wasn't too happy that you didn't join the meeting," Jack said.

"Shocker," Nick laughed. Crawford was never happy with anything Nick did. Nick didn't know if the guy was jealous because he wanted to fly all around the world, or if it was just Nick's charming personality that made Crawford not like him, but either way, he was always salty. Nick had never gone out of his way to change that so that probably played a part in it. "Give me the short version."

"Well the short version is that Crawford doesn't want you involved in the trafficking situation. He says that is the FBI's job, and that you are part of the CIA to fight terrorism. Not small-time crime."

"I'm assuming you told him I don't give a baby sheep's shit what he wants?"

Jack frowned. "I used a little more class, but yes, I let him know."

"Good. So what'd you come up with?"

"As usual Crawford won't spare an agent for one of your side projects, but he will let the FBI know that you are getting involved if you like."

"No," Nick kept it short.

"Okay."

"I don't need him. Brooke already reached out to the local FBI office in Atlanta. I got it handled. I just wanted to make sure Crawford knew all projects were paused until I see this through."

"He said you had two days," Jack said.

"And I'm assuming—"

"Yes, Nick. I told him you'd be taking as long as you wanted."

Nick reached down and patted Jack on the back. "See bud, I knew we'd make a good team."

"Yes, you piss everyone off, then they take it out on me. Great team."

"Every team has role players, Jacky. They are all just as important as the star player."

Jack walked over to the Humvee sleigh, ignoring Nick's jab. "Your coordinates are set for Kevin Swayne's address. You're sure this is the best thing to do? Pop in on a famous actor with millions of social media followers? He could blow your cover with one Tweet."

Nick walked over and climbed inside the sleigh. "Well, I don't really know what the hell a *tweet* is, but I assure you he won't be telling anyone anything when I'm done with him. Besides, I'm Santa Claus. He starts telling people I'm a covert agent instead of a toy deliverer, they'll throw him in the looney bin."

Saint Nick 2

The reindeer were ready to go. When Nick had the old rail sleigh upgraded to the Humvee, he also did away with the reins system. Zeke installed tiny speakers on the outside of the browband on the reindeer's bridles attached to their heads. The mic was always on in the Humvee so now he only had to give commands to make them move.

"All right my friends. Let's go get some bad guys."

The reindeer moved forward out of the hangar. Zeke had installed a responsive drive system on the Humvee whenever the reindeer were hooked up to the front. The sensors allowed the Humvee to automatically move with them—roll forward when they moved forward, brake when they slowed down. When Nick had suggested making the sleigh a Humvee, it was really a joke, but Zeke said the weight wouldn't matter to the reindeer. Just something else that couldn't be explained outside of the North Pole.

Either way, Nick loved his new ride, but he did not love where his ride was taking him. Thus was life for him. Never too far from the darkness of life, no matter how bright the lights around him. He had a sinking feeling this particular mission would be darker than most.

4

Nick sat forward in his seat as the reindeer wound around a few houses in an ultra posh neighborhood in the Buckhead area of Atlanta, Georgia. As he always did, he'd enabled the cloaking device when they left the North Pole so they could move around the city without being detected. It was by far his favorite Santa power other than the All Seeing Eye. To be able to move about the enemy undetected was something he would have killed for back in his Army Ranger days. And he always took full advantage of it now. As long as he kept the key fob with him, he could stay invisible to the naked eye no matter where he went.

Nick had checked the mini-ASE in the Humvee on the way to Kevin Swayne's house. Kevin was still taking calls in his office, but none of the rest of those conversations were about trafficking teenage girls. Nick slid out of the Humvee and walked over to the front door of Kevin's mansion. He looked back over his shoulder to make sure the reindeer were still cloaked, an old habit he couldn't seem to break, no matter how much he knew the cloaking device never failed.

Saint Nick 2

He walked up to the front door and rang the doorbell. A few seconds later, A-list actor, Kevin Swayne himself answered the door. He was befuddled when he didn't see anyone standing there, and he stepped out of the door to take a better look. His door still open behind him. Kevin was one of the few actors who'd managed to have a long and storied career in Hollywood. He'd been in blockbuster movies spanning over three decades. Classics—some of the best movies ever made. Staring him in the face was almost surreal to Nick, and he wasn't even a fan. The icon had salt and pepper hair, and Nick could see now that he'd had some work done to keep his face camera worthy, but it was done well.

"Hello?" Kevin said one last time.

Nick slipped around him and moved inside the house. He'd used this trick dozens of times in the past couple years. Ringing the doorbell and making like a gust of wind inside the door was easier than trying to break in. Kevin finally gave up and walked back inside. It was just the two of them now. Kevin was muttering to himself that he needed to get the gate checked. Little did he know the gate worked fine, Nick and his reindeer just had the ability to drop in without using it. Outside the neighborhood, the FBI was waiting for incriminating words. Brooke had set that up. Zeke was patching the audio to them so that they could move in if Kevin gave him what they needed.

Nick followed Kevin back to his office. Inside there were rows of movie posters on the wall, and trophies of the actors many accomplishments scattered about the cherry-wood furnishings. Kevin picked up the phone and pressed a button.

"Sorry about that. Thought someone was at the door. Anyway, send the script to my agent. If it passes his test, I'll have a look at it. You know that's how it always works." A pause. "Right. You got it." Then he hung up the phone.

Nick wandered the room while Kevin muttered some choice words about the person on the other end of the call under his breath. Nick was excited. He absolutely loved this part of being Santa Claus. The shock and awe of the person he messed with while he was invisible never got old. But he was tired of the same old tricks. Kevin Swayne was an actor of the highest regard, so he deserved a performance.

Nick was standing at the back of the office—about twenty feet from where Kevin Hollywood sat at his desk.

"I'm disappointed in you, Kevin," Nick said in his most Godly baritone voice.

Kevin fell backward in his chair he was so startled. He scrambled back to his feet and stood behind his chair like it was an iron shield. But he didn't say anything. Nick was trying to hold it together, but that was about the most dramatic reaction he'd seen to the invisible man trick. Of course, he shouldn't be surprised.

Nick spoke again. "I had such high hopes for you. I have given you so much success. And this is how you repay me!"

Nick took a few steps closer. He could see that Kevin was visibly trembling.

"Who—who the hell are you!" Kevin shouted. But still he cowered behind his chair.

"I am your maker." Nick played it up. "And because of your transgressions, I've come to take it all away."

Nick hoped Brooke and Zeke were watching on camera. They both would get a kick out of this one. He didn't know why he hadn't played God before. It was brilliant. Especially to a scumbag like Kevin involved with trafficking young girls. His conscience would make him believe almost anything.

"I—I've got a gun!"

Nick walked over to one of the trophy shelves closest to the door. He wanted to be ready when Kevin made a break for it. They always did. Nick reached out and dragged his hand along the shelf, knocking several of the priceless awards over and crashing to the floor as he belted out, "And I have omnipotent power!"

The terrified look on Kevin's face as he watched his awards fall was so satisfying. Then he made a break for the door. Nick took two power steps forward and lowered his shoulder. He connected hard to Kevin's chest and he knocked him completely off his feet, and slammed him into the wall behind him. It made a Kevin-sized impression in the drywall.

Nick toggled the cloaking device off and appeared before Kevin, standing directly over him. Kevin was startled and pulled himself back against the wall.

"All right, enough fun and games," Nick said as he folded his arms across his chest. "I know what you're involved in so don't insult me by playing dumb. If I can make myself invisible, I can figure out that you're diddling little kids. So let me be clear. I'll kill you right here, right now, with my bare hands if you don't tell me *everything* you know."

All the color drained from Kevin's face. He looked like a man who knew his life was over. Whether Nick took it from him right then or not. He either didn't want to speak, or couldn't, but either way it wasn't working for Nick. Nick stepped forward with his left foot and kicked Kevin in the chest. He doubled over and lay on his stomach as he coughed.

"Now is not the time for silence. I know there is a handoff happening tonight. Tell me where, or you're dead.

I'm not saying it again. Maybe if you sing now, the FBI will be lenient. I hope not, but it is your only chance."

Nick took a step forward. This time he was going to kick him in the head. But Kevin threw up his hand, scrambled to an upright sitting position with his back against the wall and nodded.

"Okay," he coughed. "But there's a misunderstanding. I'm only—"

Nick punched Kevin in the forehead so hard that he went unconscious, slumping down to the floor, and his head flopped down onto his chest. Not a second later Nick could hear his phone vibrating in his pocket. He didn't have to look to see who it was, he knew it was Brooke. He knew she wouldn't approve of his tactics of being physical before having hard evidence. But Nick had heard all he needed to. He answered the phone.

"I'm a little busy sweetheart, can it wait?"

"Nick, just get the information and go. I know you get bored and this is your 'me time', but you know he has cameras. They are going to see you glitch in and out of the camera, and they are going to watch you assault him without probable cause. Sooner or later they won't be able to look the other way."

"Darling. Isn't that why we decided to work with the CIA? So they could clean up the messes?"

Kevin began to stir in front of him.

"Just hurry it up. And bring some Chick-fil-A back on your way home. I'll text you the order."

Nick smiled. She was perfect for him. Even in moments as tense and serious as the one he was in, Brooke was able to keep her sense of humor and not let it change her. It took a special kind of person to be able to do this, and she was beyond that.

"Any sauces?" Nick laughed.

Brooke ended the call.

"Okay douchebag," Nick said to Kevin as he bent down and tilted up his head by his chin so that Kevin could look him in the eye. "Time to talk or the next thing I hit you with, you won't wake up."

"Midnight. Hector Ramirez is receiving three girls taken from the homeless shelter."

"There you go ladies and gentlemen, come on in," Nick said to the FBI listening in. Then he reached down and lifted Kevin up by his shirt. "Shows over for you. Turns out they've been watching you for a while now. Prisoners don't take too kindly to perverts like you who violate children. Hope they don't go easy on you."

Kevin was speechless. Nick wanted to take his frustrations with the situation out on Kevin even further, but now he had to get moving on the real problem. The people actually taking the girls in the first place. He'd save all his frustrations just for Hector Ramirez.

5

"What do you mean he's nowhere on the radar?" Nick spoke to Zeke on the phone. "How is that possible? We can see everything!"

Zeke was quiet.

Nick stared out the front windshield of the Humvee down a dark alley. His vehicle was cloaked, but he'd unhooked from the reindeer a few blocks away and sent them back to the North Pole just in case shooting became involved. He didn't want his transportation getting accidentally clipped in the crossfire. His buddy Allen was in the seat next to him. Both of them were quiet as they waited for Zeke to explain why the now known criminal—Hector Ramirez—could not be found with the All Seeing Eye.

"Zeke? It's almost showtime. What's the deal?"

"I've been looking for over an hour," Zeke's voice came through the Humvee's speakers. "And I'm telling you, there's nothing. No sign of him."

A cold chill ran down Nick's spine. One he couldn't explain. This was the first time since acquiring the special technology from Santa that he'd felt something like this.

Saint Nick 2

Like *he* was the one without the advantage. And it wasn't a good feeling. The thought occurred to him that the technology had made him complacent.

About a block and a half away, two men walked around the corner of a building under the glowing street lights in front of them. Though there was no reason to, Nick reached for the Beretta M9 at his hip. Allen noticed and shot Nick a look.

"We in trouble?"

Before Nick could answer, the two men walking toward them both simultaneously reached inside their coats. Nick started the Humvee and threw it in reverse. He had no idea how these men knew Nick and Allen were there, but they did. Bullets began to fly.

Nick stomped the gas pedal to the floor and the Humvee jerked backward as the engine roared. The bullets were coming in three round bursts. As a former Ranger, Nick immediately recognized them as being M4 Carbines. The cold chill returned for a second time. The M4 was a distinctly American gun. Nick didn't know what the hell he'd driven into, but he couldn't worry about it until he got himself and Allen out of there alive.

"M4's?" Allen shouted. He'd recognized the same thing.

It wasn't the two men shooting at them that worried Nick. Zeke had the Humvee uniquely bulletproofed. It was the two vans that had just screeched to a halt behind him, blocking the alley, and their escape, that had him concerned. These men knew that he and Allen were there in the Humvee, even though they were invisible to the naked eye.

"Zeke, we've been setup!" Nick shouted as he slammed on the brakes and jerked the Humvee into drive. He accelerated forward, right for the two men at the end of the alley in

23

front of him. He glanced in the rearview mirror and watched under a streetlight as the van doors opened and a few more men stepped out. That's when he could finally see how they knew his invisible vehicle was there, because he could see the goggles strapped to their heads under the glowing streetlight.

"They have infrared goggles on!" Nick shouted as he drove into the gunfire from the two men standing on the corner in front of him. "They knew we were coming, and they were told about our technology!"

Nick steered the Humvee right at the gunmen. When they noticed their bullets having zero effect on the Humvee, they dove out of the way at the last second to avoid becoming hood ornaments. That's when the open end of the alley that was behind them closed, the same way the one behind them had, with two vans shutting down the road. The entire thing had been orchestrated.

Nick didn't slow down.

"Hang on!" Nick shouted.

Out of the corner of his eye he watched Allen's arm shoot to the "oh shit" bar above the door and grip for dear life. Just before impact Nick glanced at the driver's side window of the van on his left. He flipped on his headlights, illuminating a man wearing the same goggles as all the others. Nick couldn't believe his eyes.

The Humvee thumped both front-ends of the roadblock vans and bounced them both backward out into the street as they crashed through. The impact for Nick and Allen wasn't too bad because of the couple foot gap between the two vans. They shot through the other side to a chorus of twisted metal and busted lights. Nick wheeled right as he surged out onto the main road.

"That could have been a lot worse," Allen said as he exhaled.

Nick checked his rearview mirror and watched the first two vans they'd almost backed into earlier come racing out through the gap his Humvee had made.

"It ain't over yet."

Allen turned in his seat to get a better look. "What the hell did we just step into?"

"A trap."

"No shit, Sherlock," Allen laughed. "Who'd you piss off?"

Nick swerved right to turn onto a cross street. He dodged a slow moving truck and ran through a red light. The vans were still on their tail.

"Who haven't I pissed off?" Nick wheeled left, running up on the median to avoid a slow-moving sedan.

Allen's question sent Nick's brain spinning through a mental Rolodex of just exactly who might want to flip on him. Nick meant it when he rhetorically asked who he'd pissed off, but to anger someone to the extent of trying to have him killed was another level.

Nick needed to leave the whodunnits for later. His hands were full with shedding the hired guns on their heels. His choice in vehicle for the new sleigh wasn't built for high speed chases through city streets. He needed to find a corner he could disappear into. But he really needed to lose the concrete. However, he was in the middle of the city.

"Piedmont Park," Allen spoke up.

"What?"

"Go to Piedmont Park. Lose them off-road. Make a right here!"

Allen and Nick were on the same page. Nick made the right and remembered that the sprawling park in the middle of Midtown was just a couple of blocks away. The vans weren't losing any ground.

"Left!" Allen shouted.

Nick turned and saw the trees come into view. The street was coming to an end in front of them. Dead ending into the park. The signs were telling him to turn right or left, but the bullets that were now bouncing off the back of the Humvee were saying drive straight through the sidewalk.

Nick pressed the gas and as the Humvee surged, Allen braced for a bumpy ride.

"Zeke, I need the reindeer at the south end of the park. Prep them for the running start like we practiced."

The tree-line was only a half a block away now.

"But we've never got that one to work!" Zeke came back. "We can't try that now!"

"Little buddy, we don't really have a choice."

Nick found a small break in the trees and steered the Humvee toward it. Beneath their fat tires, the sidewalk bumped, and for a moment, they were airborne. The concrete gave way to a steep drop that led down to the rolling hills of the park. The front-end of the Humvee pitched forward, and after a second of stomach drop, it slammed into the dirt, bounced, and corrected itself as the truck spun sideways in the grass trying to gain traction.

With a glance to the rearview, he saw the vans behind him hadn't hesitated to follow. However, their landing wasn't quite as graceful.

"Follow this around to the left," Allen pointed at the headlight lit hill in front of them.

"Zeke, we good to go?" Nick said.

"They'll be there. But Boss—,"

"Nope. Don't need your negativity, Z-man. Not now."

Zeke didn't continue his protest. Nick was fully aware of

the failures of their practice runs on this rolling start. He didn't need further reminding. As they wound around the hill the park opened up. It was flat terrain in front of them and Nick steered the Humvee left until his compass in the dash read South.

"Zeke didn't sound too confident," Allen said. "Should I be worried?"

"Yes." Nick didn't mince words.

In the distance he could see that ethereal green and purple sparkle in the sky that first caught his eye in the Iraqi desert two years ago when Santa had broken through the atmosphere. He knew without asking that the reindeer had made it.

But that was the easy part.

It was linking up with the reindeer without stopping that in trial had been nothing short of a disaster. And that was without two armed vans chasing close behind.

6

The middle of Piedmont Park was pitch black. The Humvee's headlights only illuminated more grass in front of them as the tires chewed through the manicured grounds. As the Humvee bumped and rumbled over the undulating park, Nick strained his eyes to see where the reindeer had landed, but had yet to find them.

"You do know what you're doing right?" Allen said. His voice steady in the face of danger. A constant that Nick had always found comforting.

"Sure," Nick lied. When in doubt, exude confidence.

"Shit."

His old friend knew better.

Nick moved the Humvee left around a cluster of trees. Once passed, far off in the distance he caught his first glimpse of the rope lighting he'd had Zeke run along the harnesses of the reindeer. Just for emergencies like this one.

"Showtime, Zeke!" Nick said. Then he pushed a button on the dash that brought up a camera. It was showing the hitch at the front of the Humvee.

Saint Nick 2

"I've started the reindeer forward," Zeke's voice came through the speakers.

"Can't you just stop and link up, then get going again, Nick?" Brooke's worried voice followed Zeke's from the War Room back at the NP.

"Not now, babe. Got two bogeys hot on my six. No time to stop."

"Nick you're going to get yourself or those reindeer hurt, or worse if you do this. I know I don't have to remind you of what happened last time you tried this—"

Nick ended the call. They were closing in on the reindeer and he had to focus.

"Nicky," Allen said. "What the hell happened last time you tried this?"

"Not now, bud."

"Great. I always thought I'd die in a firefight or stepping on a IED. Nope. I'm gonna die beside Santa Claus trying to hitch to the sleigh being pulled by reindeer."

"Allen. Please. I've got to slow down. I need you to hold the vans back as they catch up."

Nick pressed a button and the rear windshield popped outward in the SUV's back gate.

"Roger that," Allen said as he climbed to the back.

Nick focused forward. He let off the gas and coasted as he failed at trying not to remember what Brooke was about to remind him of—the faulty last attempt at this running start at a connection. It was hard not to picture the way he had to swerve the Humvee away so hard at the last minute that it flipped over on its side. It was his only option because if he'd hit the back of the sleigh at the speed he'd been going, it would have pushed forward too hard and broken some precious reindeer legs.

They figured out that they had to have the sleigh hooked

up to the reindeer to make this moving connection work, because it was the only way to have a steady hitch on the back. If done right, it will link into place and the reindeer will pull away with the Humvee in neutral, off to the happy place in the great North. The stakes were even higher now. If the same thing happened this time and the Humvee overturned, the reindeer would likely be shot, and Nick and Allen would have to make a stand just the two of them. Unkind odds even in perfect conditions.

Allen began firing at the vans out the open rear windshield. The sound was louder than Nick expected inside the truck. With each round he jerked, making it even harder to concentrate on the task in front of him. Nick had slowed the Humvee to around twenty miles-per-hour, letting the deceleration happen naturally as he watched the sleigh pull forward in front of him. Zeke coached the reindeer to pull to about ten miles-per-hour until they felt the Humvee bump the sleigh. They had then been taught to take off, regardless of if the Humvee had actually linked up or not. It was the last ditch safety valve for the most precious animals in all the world.

"They just keep coming, Nick! I can't see shit!" Allen shouted in between shots.

"It's go time, Al. Strap in brother!"

Just in front of him now, Nick watched the rope lights bob up and down with the reindeer's movement. Zeke had installed a small spotlight on the back of the sleigh that shone down on the hitch. It was like a beacon for the front end of the Humvee now. Nick let the Humvee idle a bit more as it coasted forward he was at about fifteen miles-per-hour and looked to be perfectly centered.

Allen looked back over his shoulder as he clicked his seatbelt. They're closing fast, Nick. They're gonna catch up!"

Saint Nick 2

Nick had about a hundred yards to go. But from the looks of it, the vans were merely feet from his back end. He wasn't going to make it. He was going to have to speed up.

Nick clicked on his earpiece. It was tuned only to the reindeer. "I need a little more guys. You hear me? Gimme more speed!"

A spray of bullets clanked against the bulletproof rear windshield, and more gunfire could be heard clapping into the night over the Humvee's engine. Nick pressed the gas down a little and the speedometer rose to twenty miles-per-hour. The Humvee's speaker system beeped and Brooke's voice boomed inside the truck.

"You're going to get them all killed, Nick! You're going too fast! It will never work!"

This time it was Allen who ended the call with the North Pole by punching a button on the dash.

"Don't listen to her, Nick. You got this."

It was a valiant gesture by Allen, but Nick had already tuned it out. He had one mind, and it was on the little light shining over the hitch. Any outside interference at this point was going to fall on deaf ears. He was ready to connect to that sleigh.

Nick could tell the reindeer had done what he'd asked because he was barely catching them at eighteen miles-per-hour. He was just a few feet away now. He was going to make it.

"We're running out of park grounds here bud. It's now or never!"

Nick heard Allen, but he couldn't take his eyes off the back of the sleigh. He pressed the gas a little more and pushed forward. He was lined up just right. Just a little more speed and he was going to fit it right in.

Inches from linking with the sleigh—less than a foot

away—the back end of the Humvee bounced upward and a loud bang filled the air around them. Someone from the vans had shot out a back tire, and it was just as Nick was pulling into place. When the back end sat back down, the impact spun the steering wheel in his hand and the Humvee veered right.

"Abort, Nick! Abort!"

Nick glanced in the side mirror as he jerked the steering wheel back to the right. The van behind him was so close it might as well have been inside the Humvee with them.

"Just pull away, Nick!" Allen shouted again as he grabbed for his rifle.

But Nick had no thoughts of pulling away. He saw the streetlights in front of the reindeer growing dangerously close. They were going to have to pull up, whether Nick and Allen were coming along with them or not. If Nick didn't connect, there would be no getting away with a flat tire.

Nick gave the gas one last push and steered toward the back end of the sleigh. He could see that it had pitched upward, which meant the reindeer had begun to leave the ground. The Humvee wobbled wildly as he pressed forward, bouncing him to the left and to the right of the hitch. He was close enough now that all he had to rely on was the camera on the dash.

"Now, Nick!"

Nick swerved left and punched the gas. He'd hit the pedal harder than he wanted to and shoved into the back of the sleigh. Before he could really see if he was connected, the front end of the Humvee jerked upward. And just like that, the violent encounter was over. The lights of the vans moved farther and farther away, and then so too did the big city lights. After a celebratory fist bump with his old friend, there was a moment where eating cookies and delivering presents didn't sound so bad after all. But as they pushed through the clouds on their way to safety, Nick realized those kids down there in reality didn't have a magical ride to safety like he did. And because of that, he wouldn't consider quitting on them ever again.

7

"I have a business to run!" Hector Ramirez slammed his fist down on the desk in front of him.

Wealthy businessman and oil tycoon, Jack Frost, was not impressed. Jack turned his wheelchair toward the tall window at the back of his office and wheeled over to it. When Jack was just a boy, his parents left him for dead one freezing night in the middle of a Montana snowstorm. Ever since that night, his legs were useless, and many would say, so was his heart.

Jack's connections run deep in all circles of the world. The government, big business, and many of the darker corners as well. In each of these different parts of society, he is widely known as ruthless—a man who gets what he wants and doesn't care who he steps on. All his life he's been using these connections to pad his pockets, all for the day when he could begin to go to work on what he really wanted out of life—for everyone to suffer as greatly as he had. Jack liked who he had become, and he attributed all his success to the horrifying childhood he'd survived.

Jack now believed in order to build a more successful

society, there needed to be more men and women like him. He felt the only way to get that done was to ruin as many childhoods as he possibly could. From there, he knew the cream would rise to the top, just as he had. His way of starting this, was working with scumbags like Hector Ramirez. A man who was one of the very best at ruining childhoods. Hector achieved this through buying and selling children to even bigger scumbags who were willing to pay lots of money for the privilege. What happened to the children once they were sold, was of no concern to Jack, just as long as it taught them how horrid the world can be, and how to rise above it. Those were the future leaders Jack wanted to surround himself with, and this was the way to do it.

"Are you listening to me old man?" Hector shouted.

Jack turned to face the small Mexican man. "Are you finished?"

Hector let out a huff of frustration and put his hands on his hips. "I don't understand what chasing this guy has to do with making money!"

"That's why you're not in charge, Hector. Because you are too stupid to see even one step ahead."

Hector stared at Jack like a deer in headlights.

Almost two years ago, when Jack first heard whispers of a man named Nick Campos, from the highest and most top secret positions within the government's most elite defense agencies, Jack had become obsessed. He used every contact he'd ever procured to obtain information that no other civilian had. The wild tales that were swirling about the "invisible man" with the sleigh, and all other forms of nonsense simply astounded him. The more he dove in, the more he learned.

They called the man Saint Nick in the back rooms of the

CIA. The notion of an actual Santa Claus drove Jack so unbelievably mad that all other goals nearly ceased to exist, except finding that man. He wasn't sure if his obsession stemmed from his hatred for anyone who actually coddled and spoiled children, or if it was just the thought of having a real-life archenemy that intrigued him so, but whatever it was, he was relentless in his pursuit. He had always been a fan of superhero comic books—the villains to be more precise. They were always smarter than the do-no-wrong good guy. Jack could relate to that. And reading those comics over and over hiding from the next beating his dad gave him was the only thing that got him through his horrid childhood. And now that he'd finally found what could be his own rival, he wasn't going to let Hector—the small-time criminal—ruin his chance living out the fantasies of his youth.

"This man sniffed out our little trap I set just as I told you he would. So do you understand what that means Mr. Ramirez?"

Again, all Jack got was a blank stare.

"I'll keep it simple, then you can just go back to doing what the hell I tell you to do. It means the man who flew off unexplainably into the sky just a bit ago, him and everyone he knows at the FBI and the CIA is onto your little operation."

"You mean *our* operation, Mr. Frost."

Jack uncoiled a crooked smile. "No, Hector. I mean *your* operation. I could just serve you up to these people on a platter. I have dozens of other men like you operating for me all across the country. It's cliche, but you need me, I don't need you."

Hector's posture seemed to resign himself to the fact that this was true.

"However," Jack wheeled closer to Hector. "If you want to remain in operation, you'll focus all of your resources on helping me get rid of this problem. I have a couple of other ventures that are in need of new management. You show me you can do this for me, and I will take very good care of you."

Hector seemed to like the thought of this. Just as Jack knew he would. Years of business taught Jack a lot of things, none more important than that of the dangling carrot. Make it look tasty enough and they'll chase it till their death.

"So what now? The guy can fly? How we supposed to fight that?"

"Your first good question, Hector. For now, just keep your radio jammers on you. You lose those, and he will find you. Understand?"

"Whatever you say."

"Just stay ready. I'll have something for you in the morning."

Hector and his men left Jack's office. Jack wheeled back over to his desk where footage of the night's adventure were playing on all three of his monitors. He'd had drones recording every move the entire time. He knew if he studied long enough, he would find a weakness. Then he would exploit it. It's what he did best.

8

Of no surprise to Nick, snow was falling when they arrived back at the North Pole. After making sure the reindeer were all right, he and Allen made the short walk from the barn to Nick's house. The gingerbread looking home still had the lights on inside. Nick hoped Brooke wouldn't be sore about how he couldn't respond to her during the action earlier.

Nick and Allen walked in and the warmth hugged them inside the door. The house smelled of cooked meat—steak if Nick's nose was on it's game. That had to be a good sign. Then Brooke rounded the corner from the kitchen wearing a stern look that suggested maybe he was wrong about that sign.

"Just who the hell do you think you are ignoring your wife like that?" She was stomping toward him. Allen took a step away from Nick like he didn't want to be guilty by association. Nick was royally confused. This couldn't be less like the woman he'd just married.

"I—" Nick stopped his attempt to explain when Brooke's scowl turned into a smile. Then she began to laugh.

"You should have seen your face, Nick. Come on. I was an FBI agent. You don't think I understand how it goes out there in the field?"

The tension fell from Nick's shoulders as he smiled.

"I should never have gotten involved," Brooke continued. "That was the last thing you needed in the moment. So I made you boys some ribeyes. Medium rare, just how you like them."

Brooke waved them toward the kitchen. They both followed.

"You had me worried there for a minute, Brookie," Allen said.

"You're not the only one," Nick laughed. "But, I have to get out to the War Room, honey. Somebody set us up. We—"

"Zeke and I are all over it," Brooke interrupted. She picked up a few Tupperware containers. She'd already packed the steaks to go. She knew Nick would want to get right out and stay on the case. "I've been backchanneling my FBI and CIA contacts. There's a leak somewhere and we need to plug it up."

Nick grunted with satisfaction. "If there wasn't somebody trying to kill me right now, I'd take you upstairs and—"

"Eh-ehm," Allen cleared his throat.

Brooke gave Nick a devilish grin as she moved past him toward the door. Allen gave Nick a wink and a hard slap on the back. The three of them made the short but chilly walk to the War Room where Zeke was hard at work over at the monitors.

"Anything new?" Brooke asked him.

Zeke turned and hopped off his chair. Nick looked down at his little buddy. He looked tired. His fuzzy brown hair was a mess and his beard had some sort of cake crumbs still tucked inside.

"Good to see you boss. That was quite the exit earlier." He turned to Brooke. "Nothing. I've got nothing on all known associates to Hector Ramirez. It's like they all just up and disappeared."

The four of them were quiet for a moment. They all looked at each other knowingly. This was no coincidence. Nick knew what they were thinking. Just like Nasir Samara had learned to use the frequency jammer to stay off the All Seeing Eye's radar last Christmas, someone had tipped Hector Ramirez to do the same. But something wasn't adding up for Nick. It wasn't until just yesterday that Nick even knew who the hell Hector Ramirez was, so how could he possibly know, or even want to hide from Nick?

Nick looked at Zeke. "You haven't found anything, because you weren't looking in the right place. Now that we know we were setup, we have to think differently."

"Different how?" Allen asked.

"We're going to have to use some old school investigative work," Nick said as he smiled at Brooke.

"Why?" Zeke said. "We have the ASE. We can just listen in on anyone."

"That's exactly what got us into this mess," Nick said.

Zeke looked confused.

"Where you going with this?" Brooke said.

"This entire thing started with Kevin Swayne, right?"

"Right," Zeke answered.

"The actor." Nick let that hang in the air for a minute.

"You think he was acting?" Brooke said.

"Sort of. I think he's the scumbag the conversation we listened in on made him sound like, so that part was true.

But I think he was putting on for us. I think we were meant to hear that conversation so I would jump into action."

"I don't get it," Allen said. "Why would an A-list actor incriminate himself in such a way, just to get Combat Santa Claus to come down and bust him?"

"That's why we're going to have to investigate. The ASE can't see into the past. So we are going to have to find out why he would do such a thing. But it's the only thing that makes sense. It obviously isn't Hector Ramirez that is after me. He's just a pawn. The crux of this entire thing is figuring out who's moving the chess pieces."

"Where do we start with that?" Zeke asked. Way out of his league.

Brooke answered for Nick. "Has to be someone on the inside. At least the leak has to be. There's no other way someone would know how to see you while you're cloaked."

"Good thing we have a resident FBI investigator," Nick said to Brooke. "What do you say you put on your old pants suit special agent? Maybe go kick some tires in the morning."

Brooke's face lit up. Nick had been suspecting that she'd been growing bored stuck here in Winter Wonderland. Her look of excitement confirmed it.

"I'll make a run down to the States first thing in the morning," Brooke said. "In the meantime, let me have an hour or two on the ASE to look around while you guys get some rest. I have a few ideas of where to start."

Brooke opened the Tupperware and the scent of buttered red meat wafted Nick's way. "Twist my arm," he said.

No arm twisting was necessary.

9

Sleep didn't come easy for Nick that night. The bourbon lowered his anxiety but only increased the tossing and turning. Morning came slow, but when it did he was ready to make some moves. Brooke left early with the reindeer. She was headed for FBI headquarters in Washington, DC. She had an old friend who was high up the ranks and she figured that was as good a place as any to start asking questions. But something was gnawing at Nick. And whatever it was led him to believe that Brooke's trip wouldn't yield any significant results.

Nick was currently running the boardwalk at Clearwater Beach, Florida. He wasn't actually there, but the contraption some of the elves had built for him because they knew he liked to jog was an outstandingly close second. Instead of having to wear VR goggles, they made a room in his gym out of screens. All he had to do was punch in the location he wanted to run, and the connected All Seeing Eye used its technology to completely recreate the exact route. Complete with the awe-inspiring sunrise, and even the passed out homeless man by the beach trash cans. The smell of ocean being pumped in via "AccScent Technology" was the icing on the cake. Zeke had put his magic touch on that one.

Unfortunately, the run was dampened by the heaviness of what had happened last night. His operation was in danger of being outed across the world if Nick didn't find out who was onto him. And worse, he couldn't stop the human trafficking ring if he couldn't see where they were operating. Brooke had left a morbid note that three more young women were taken late in the night. Salt on the wound of an already stinging morning.

As Nick passed Post Corner Pizza—one of his favorite pizza places—on his virtual run, that gnawing feeling came back and bit him so hard he shut down the treadmill and hopped off. As he watched the waves crash against the video beach in the distance, his first encounter with civilians as Santa Claus a year ago flooded back to him. More importantly, the way he had embarrassed Jim Calipari, head of the FBI's Los Angeles division played in his mind. Nick already hated Jim for stealing his girl back in college, so the way Nick treated him that day was especially harsh. Nick didn't know why he thought of Jim and how they had gone at it in a moment when he was trying to figure out who might have snitched on Nick's current situation, but he did, and he couldn't put the rabbit back in the hat. He had to talk to Brooke.

There was a knock at the door. Brooke walked in.

"Think of the devil and she shall appear."

"Huh?"

"Never mind," Nick said as he wiped the sweat from his forehead with a towel. "Did you forget something?"

"Already been and just got back."

"That was quick."

Brooke came over and gave him a kiss. "Yeah, Anne and I

didn't get past catching up before I had to get back here. I was going to call, but thought we may as well talk in person."

"Well this can't be good. What happened?"

Nick walked over and took a seat on the fly machine. Brooke sat beside him on the weight bench.

"So Anne and I were saying our hello's when about two minutes in she perked up and asked if I had heard about Jim Calipari."

Nick's stomach dropped. He couldn't believe she'd just mentioned Jim's name.

"What?" Brooke said. "Why the look?"

"Go on. I'll tell you in a minute," Nick shook his head as he rubbed the scruff on his chin.

Brooke gave him an upturned eyebrow then moved on. "Apparently, not long after the new year, he started being flaky with the Bureau. Not showing up on time. Missing meetings. Poorly coordinating strikes and so on. So much so that they fired him."

"Okay, odd maybe, but hardly something to stop your investigation short this morning to come back here."

"Getting there. Anne said that one of her contacts in Los Angeles was having lunch when he showed up."

Nick made a "wow" face.

Brooke rolled her eyes. "Would you just let me finish? It was noteworthy because he was having lunch with that rich guy, Jack Frost."

"The oil guy?"

"Yeah," Brooke said.

"Okay. I don't get it. Who cares?"

"Well she said her friend just thought it was weird, but it got weirder when she saw him drive away in his own Lamborghini."

Saint Nick 2

"Baby, why is this relevant? So what? He got a job for some rich dude. Probably doing security or something. Good for him. I hope he dies with a bunch of toys."

"That's the thing, Nick. He doesn't have a job. Anne said her friend is the nosey type. Doesn't help that she's an investigator by trade. But she looked him up. Jim doesn't have an employment status. And he doesn't live in California anymore. He bought a mansion just outside Mexico City. No one has seen or heard from him since."

"Yeah, that is weird. But what does that have to do with us? You think because he lives in Mexico he works for some slave trade now? That's a little racist don't you think?"

Nick meant the jab to lighten her mood, but Brooke, as usual, didn't find him amusing. She stood and started walking for the door.

"Come on, Brooke. It was just a joke. I'm just saying I don't see the connection."

"Of course because he lives in Mexico now, by itself, doesn't mean he works for traffickers. But the fact that he is suddenly filthy rich, doesn't have a job, lives in Mexico, and, oh by the way, totally hates you . . . Yeah, that raises more than one red flag with me. It doesn't you?"

It actually did. Especially since he'd already had the son of a bitch on his mind while on the treadmill.

Nick stood and walked over to her. "The reason I gave you that look earlier when you mentioned his name was because for some strange reason, I was thinking about last year too. And how Jim is one of the only people on the planet that knows about me. How much we hate each other crossed my mind too, I just hadn't made the leap yet that he could be connected."

"What about now?" Brooke asked.

"Yeah. Now I'm thinking about it. And I don't like it."

Brooke opened the door. "I'm going to hit the ASE and see if we can find what Jim is up to. And while I'm at it, I'll check on that Jack Frost guy too. Probably just a coincidence, but no harm in seeing if there's any connection back in the bank records anywhere."

"You're sexy when you're on the hunt." Nick flashed her a smile.

"You're hormones flare when you get shot at. We're a mess, but we're perfect for each other."

10

Nick couldn't just sit around and wait for information to get back to him. He didn't know how long it would be before Brooke could tie Jim to this thing—*if* she could even tie him to it at all. So he had to go and control what he could. Brooke had put in a request to talk to Kevin Swayne so they could try to get answers on who hired him. *If* someone had hired him. There were a lot of if's going around. But the red tape of an outsider without any credentials getting in to talk to him would also take some time. And after trying to key in on the three girls who went missing overnight in Atlanta, and not being able to, just like he couldn't find Hector Ramirez, he knew the two had to be connected.

Nick had sent one of his faithful elves down to rent a car. About six months ago he tried this but the elf wasn't allowed a rental without a driver's license, and, well, an ID at all for that matter. So Nick made sure he got citizenship for one of the elves just for situations like this one. Henry had successfully rented Nick an unassuming Nissan Maxima, and on the corner of Maryland Circle and University Avenue, Nick was watching the outside of a truck service shop. Brooke had found that Hector had been seen there on more than one occasion, and the business just so happened to be under ownership of a José Ramirez. Hector's older brother. Nick guessed that Hector, and whoever was in charge of him hadn't counted on anyone doing any actual investigative work. Or maybe they had and were ready for someone to come snooping. But that's why Nick brought Allen.

"Well, I see a lot of Mexicans loitering around the building," Allen said. "Probably a good chance we're in the right spot."

"Well, a Mexican man does own the place Al."

"Touché. What's the play? It's the middle of the day. We going in cloaked or what?"

Nick reached back to the back seat and dove his hand down inside the big red sack. Other than the ability to fly around the world in seconds, this was Nick's favorite of Santa's tricks he'd left behind.

Allen glanced back over his shoulder. "How is this real life? Still feels like a bad story while we are drunk, or I'm going to wake up back in Kuwait or something."

Nick understood what Allen meant. Though it had been two years now, things like reaching into a bottomless sack for whatever you desire still hadn't sunk all the way in as reality. Yet here they were.

Nick pulled a hat and button down short-sleeved shirt from his sack.

"The hell is this?" Allen took the clothing. "A disguise? Really?"

"Really."

"All this techno shit you got and we are going with disguises? Like a couple of bad detectives on a B network TV show?"

Saint Nick 2

"Think about it, Allen. Last night, they knew to use infrared to be able to see us. What makes you think that after we got away, if this is where some of Hector's men are, they wouldn't have something in there to detect us?"

Allen glanced toward the building, shrugged his shoulders, and nodded. "That's fair." Then he held up the hat. "The hell is an Xfinity?"

"Internet company," Nick said. Then he pressed the COM button on his cloaking fob.

Zeke's voice came through the small speaker at the bottom. "Internet's been down for about an hour."

Allen gave Nick a smirk.

"Perfect. Keep an eye on us. When I take my hat off, restore the internet."

"You've got it, boss. I see five men inside at the moment. But that doesn't mean there aren't more. Still no sign of Hector on the ASE. Can't see him or his most known underbosses. So they could be there, just using the frequency jammers."

"Roger that." Nick put the fob away.

"That little guy is handy as a shirt pocket, ain't he?" Allen said.

"He really is. Imagine if we'd have had little elves that could make up a disguise for us in a matter of minutes going into some of the situations we've been in."

"Would have been nice."

The two of them changed clothes and Nick grabbed the clipboard Zeke had left him. It was equipped with an Xfinity company logo and all. Nick handed Allen his technician badge.

"Not your best photo," Nick said with a laugh. The picture was an old one Nick had of his friend. One of the elves had superimposed an Xfinity hat on him. It was just enough to look legitimate.

Allen laughed when he saw the picture. "I remember this. Almost got shot that night outside of that super shady bar in Phnom Penh."

"That's because you had to hit on the only woman with a boyfriend in the entire city."

Allen laughed as he clipped the badge to his shirt. Nick did the same and they got out of the car. Other than being in better physical condition than a real technician probably would be, they both pretty much looked the part. They crossed the street and walked toward the entrance. The building was a warehouse with a makeshift storefront facing the road. There were spare car parts, tires, and all the trimmings of a beat up repair shop. It was an unseasonably warm day in Atlanta so a couple of people were sitting outside the entrance. Nick nodded a silent hello as he and Allen entered the building.

It wasn't a formal reception room by any standards. In fact, there wasn't much at all. A small desk on the left side and enough dirt and dust to choke a horse. Nick didn't know much about Hector Ramirez's brother, but from the looks of his business, it was likely more of a front for more sinister dealings than a legit repair shop. No one was inside so Nick stepped back outside and got the attention of the man sitting out front.

"Anyone working today?"

"Who's asking?" The chubby, half bald man said. And he wasn't too happy about having to say that much.

"Internet's down in the area. Just wanted to have a look and see if I could get everything back up and running."

The man perked up a bit. "Internet? Yeah, went down

about an hour ago. Don't really know what to do with myself without it."

A sad state the world had fallen into.

"Point me in a good direction?" Nick said.

The man attempted to rise from the chair twice. The third time he finally made it. Then he walked past them into the building. Nick and Allen followed. The waddling man opened another door and walked them into the garage. There were only a couple of cars inside. Two or three men wandering around them, not quite doing any work. Nick scanned the open room and all seemed legit to the naked eye. The chubby man turned right and they were walking toward what looked like a small office. There was a man sitting at a desk staring at a computer. When he looked up and noticed Nick and Allen's internet company logos, he shot up out of his chair.

"Oh thank God. That was quick. Right this way guys."

"Did it just go out on you?" Nick asked.

"Bout an hour ago. No clue what happened. We sell parts online so I need to get back on."

"Show me your wiring and we'll get you fixed up."

Just before Nick walked into the office, one of the men half-working caught his eye, then glanced quickly back down at the towel in his hand. Nick didn't like the way it happened. It was unnatural somehow. Nick was just a tech guy coming to fix a problem. Why would he be interested in Nick enough to look away hard when caught. Sure, Nick knew his striking good looks garnered attention from both men and women alike, but in this situation he doubted that's what it was. And as he walked into the office, he couldn't help but feel like they'd been setup.

Again.

11

With the thought of a setup still lingering in his mind, Nick and Allen let the man walk them into the office.

"Here you go," the office worker pointed to a cluster of modems, routers, and wires. Nick was no "techspert", but this looked like more than just a small business would need to sell a few spare parts online.

Nick knelt down and acted like he cared about the wiring. There was a door on the back wall. From his overview of the outside, there was another small warehouse he still hadn't been in yet. But the five men Zeke saw with the ASE had already been accounted for.

"Okay, anything else?" Nick said.

"This is it."

"What about back here?" Nick stepped over to the door and put his hand on the knob.

The Mexican office worker, dressed nothing like an office worker, stepped over quickly and pushed the door shut so Nick couldn't open it. That was when Nick spotted the pistol tucked into his belt.

Saint Nick 2

"Nothing back here but parts inventory."

"Oh, sorry 'bout that. I thought your central wiring came through back there."

"Nope. It's all right here."

The man's quick reaction didn't mean they were hiding anything sinister in whatever room was behind that door, but it certainly meant there was something he didn't want anyone to see. And knowing who Nick was dealing with by the bloodline of ownership, it was enough to know he had to find out what it was. The gun on his hip was just further proof that something was going on. And Nick needed to get out in front of it, if it wasn't already too late.

Nick nodded and went back to the nest of wires. He acted as though he were looking over everything as he unscrewed the coaxial cable from the back of the modem. He snapped the lone prong in half with his thumb, nosed around a little more, then *magically* found the problem. He turned back to the office worker and held up the cable.

"This probably has something to do with it."

"Damn. Didn't see that. That an easy fix?"

"Very. I have a fresh cable with my supplies in the car. I will upgrade you to our new cables while I'm at it. Make your internet faster. That work?" He went ahead and tried to sell it just in case they weren't actually being set up.

The man smiled. "Yeah man! Sounds great," he said pointing to the chubby man that walked them in. "Now there won't be a delay in Chi Chi's porn stream."

Chi Chi didn't laugh.

"All right, we can get you fixed up. Me and Al will check the box outside just to make sure all the optics look good. Then we'll replace the cables. Half hour tops."

"Just come on back when you're ready to fix these," the man said.

"Will do."

Nick nodded to Allen. He *really* didn't want to turn his back to the armed office worker, but to conceal their true intentions, he needed to act normal for just a bit longer if the situation allowed. Allen led the way back into the garage. The man who'd caught his attention earlier was actually working on an engine this time. Maybe Nick was just being paranoid. They passed through the front and both of them walked out into the sunshine.

"What's your read?" Allen said without turning around.

"They knew we might be coming." It came out without Nick knowing he even felt that way. It was a reflex.

"Then why the hell are we walking so slow back to the car?"

It was a good question. Nick wasn't sure except for the fact that he didn't want to raise any flags. They rounded the car and Nick glanced back at the building. Chi Chi and Office Gunman had walked out as if they were expecting to see something.

Expecting to see a show, Nick thought. Then he spotted a man walking around the back of the building on the right side. He was carrying a duffel bag. It could have been for a million legitimate and benign reasons, but Nick could feel it in his bones that that man had just done something Nick and Allen wouldn't like.

Nick watched Allen reach for the door handle and another reflex made Nick spring forward, grab Allen by the back of his shirt and yank him backward. If he hadn't, Allen would be dead.

The front end of the car exploded and flames erupted from under the hood. The blast blew Allen back on top of Nick. For a moment the cover of the car between them and the building full of gangsters would save them from the cleanup crew Nick knew would be coming to make sure he was dead. Nick heard Allen groan as he rolled him from on top of him, so even though the enemy almost won, Nick and Allen both survived. For the time being.

Nick's ears were ringing and he could feel his skin stinging like a ripe sunburn. Other than that, he seemed to be okay. He looked at the back seat of the car as the front-end burned. The gangsters had just made two fatal errors. The first was not making the car bomb big enough, thus allowing Nick to live. The second, and the one that was about to really cost them, was that they hadn't done anything to harm Santa's sack in the backseat. If he could make it there before the gunmen that he knew were coming made it to the car, he was going to make it rain on these sons of bitches.

Nick sat up and moved to one knee, keeping his head below the car for cover. He glanced back at Allen. Allen was writhing in pain, but he managed to wave Nick forward. Nick peeked above the flames on the hood and saw what he had expected—three men holding rifles walking his way. He duck-walked over to the rear driver's side door and pulled it open.

Loaded Barrett 50 caliber rifle, he thought. Then he reached down into the sack. It took both hands to pull the rifle out of nowhere. He chose the 50 caliber because he wanted the gunmen he hadn't shot yet to know what was coming. He wanted fear to be the last emotion before they met their maker.

Nick locked a round in the chamber as he hoisted the rifle up and rested it on the roof. He found the first target in the sights and squeezed the trigger. The boom echoed off the trees behind the building and the rifle jerked back into Nick's shoulder. The gunman in his sights lost the left side of his face for trying to kill Allen. The next two men froze in their tracks. Taking a second to look back at their disintegrated partner in crime.

"Who's next?" Nick shouted across the parking lot. "No volunteers? Okay. I'll pick!"

He moved his eye back behind the sights and shot the leg clean off the man who was running for cover. He moved the rifle a bit to the right and round the other gunman. He squeezed the trigger and eviscerated the back of the man's neck.

A couple of men walked out into the sun from the back of the warehouse where Nick and Allen hadn't been allowed to go. Nick wanted to move forward before they had a chance to make a break for it, or cover anything up they'd been hiding there. If there were vehicles on the other side of the building they would be able to get away for sure. He looked back at Allen who was just starting to sit up.

"You just going to lay there all day or are you gonna join the fun?"

"That a Barrett?" Allen grunted. Then a small grin developed.

Allen was a sniper. One of the best in Special Forces. Nick knew he wouldn't be able to resist the old girl in his hands once again. Nick pulled the rifle off the top of the car and handed it to Allen as he rose to his feet.

"Can you handle her?"

"That's overkill, Nick. Just like you to do too much." Allen bypassed Nick's offering of the Barrett rifle and went to the back seat. "Two 20 round SR-25's."

Nick watched as Allen reached into the sack and pulled out one, then two semi-automatic rifles. He turned and handed one to Nick. "These are more appropriate. Now go get these bastards before they get away."

Saint Nick 2

Nick nodded and took one of the SR-25's. Allen chose these because they were great at mid to short range, and the two of them had practiced with them often on the range in the last two months. Then Nick started around the corner of the car to go do what his friend had asked him to do. Allen was already backing up the enemy with suppressive fire.

It felt like the good old days.

12

Nick approached the back of the building with his rifle raised. He was staying low, ready to move left or right at any moment. Allen had taken out a couple of men at the front entrance that was now to Nick's left. Nick sidled up to the aluminum outside wall and pressed the call button on his key fob. The reindeer would be en route. He had instructed Zeke when he saw the call come in that he adjust their landing spot to a couple of blocks away. Cloaked of course. Which, at this point, Nick wasn't sure there was such a thing anymore. When Nick hits the button again, they will come to his exact location.

Next, Nick pressed the cloaking button for himself. He wasn't sure who was wearing infrared goggles and who wasn't, but better to be invisible to some than seen by everyone. The only downside was that Allen could no longer see him. But Allen was going to go in the front door, so it didn't matter anyway once Nick rounded the corner. Which he did with a swing of his rifle. His finger caressed the trigger as he searched, but found no one at the back.

An engine started up around the last corner. Nick

hurried forward. When he came to the edge, tires squealed as a car whipped around from reverse to facing forward. They were looking right at Nick, but couldn't see him. It was a white van. The kind you would see out and whoever you were with would say, "I bet there's a serial killer in there". Nick lowered the nose of his rifle and shot out the front two tires. The look of surprise on the driver's face was priceless when he couldn't find the shooter.

Nick moved forward toward the driver's side door. The driver jumped out and began waiving a pistol around and shouting in Spanish. Nick flipped his gun around and smacked him in the forehead with the butt. The man that had just exited the passenger side dropped his gun when he saw his buddy go down without anyone standing in front of him.

Nick uncloaked. "What's inside that hangar. Lie to me and you die. That simple."

The Mexican man searched Nick's eyes but found no way out of telling the truth. The answer rocked Nick. Later he would be able to tell you beyond the shadow of a doubt that it changed him forever.

"Girls," the man said.

Nick swallowed hard and walked around the front of the van.

"I promise, I am just drug dealer. I have nothing to do with what is going on in there."

The man was genuinely frightened.

Nick put the tip of his large rifle up to the man's chin. Urine soaked the jeans he was wearing down his left leg.

"What's in the back of the van?"

Nick decided if it was drugs, he'd let him live. But if there was a human being back there, he was going to kill him.

"Drugs. Marijuana, Molly, Oxy. That's all. Take it. I told you I am just a dealer!"

Nick looked back over his shoulder. Allen was advancing toward the front entrance. He needed to make this quick.

"Open the doors."

The man was visibly happy to do so, and right then Nick knew it would in fact be drugs. The man opened the door to confirm.

"Put your friend in the back and you get in there with him. If I come back out and you are gone..."

Nick toggled the cloaking device on and off—disappearing, then reappearing. "I'll find you. And kill you both. Understood?"

The man didn't answer, he just ran around the van and did as Nick asked.

"How many men are inside?"

The man heaved his friend up into the back beside stacks of laughy lettuce-filled bags. "I don't know. I saw two, but could be more."

Nick didn't wait for the man to shut himself inside before he cloaked and walked over to the door. He tuned his ears to the door but could see nothing. He pulled his fob from his pocket and pressed call.

"That was crazy!" Zeke shouted.

"Anything in the warehouse? Can you see at all?"

"N-nothing," Zeke said collecting himself. "If there's anyone in there, they're using a jammer."

Nick had plenty of rounds left in his rifle. This wasn't the ideal situation, but after hearing the dealer tell him there were girls inside, it wouldn't have mattered if he were there all alone. He was going in. And if they were ready with infrared goggles, then he would be going in like he would have with the Rangers, using battle tested tactics instead of Santa magic.

At the other end of the building Nick heard the distinct sound of Allen's SR-25 rattling off some fresh rounds. This was Nick's window. He tested the door, but it was locked. The keypad on the wall beside it was the only way in. He whipped his gun around and ran to the back of the van. He uncloaked, ripped open the door, and shoved his rifle in the dealer's face.

"The keypad number. Now."

More gunshots rang out from the building. Allen was taking on the entire warehouse. Nick had to move.

"Three, eight, six, three!"

Nick cloaked as he ran to the door and punched in the number. There was a loud buzz as it unlocked and he busted through the door, found a large box on his left, and dove behind it.

More gunfire.

Nick took a quick glance around. He was pretty certain his cloak wasn't working at that moment. Because right beside him was a broad range frequency jammer, and the reason the ASE couldn't see inside the building. But he remained cloaked just in case. Out in front of him there were two unattached semi-truck trailers sitting in the middle of an open warehouse. Boxes were dotted throughout the building and one man was running toward Allen's gunfire. Nick raised his weapon but resisted the urge to shoot. He needed to keep himself a secret as long as he could. He didn't see anyone else inside. Their attention had all been pulled to the front of the building.

Nick ran around the closed up trailers and on the other side was a makeshift lounge area where it looked like the men passed their time. A couple of tables and a few tv's were in front of the door Nick had tried to open in the office earlier. That door was open now, and more gunfire popped off just on the other side. That's when Nick heard the first scream. It was unmistakable. All of the noise from the guns came from the other room, so it was easy to hear the muffled shout of a girl coming from one of the trailers. Nick looked over at the trailer and his skin crawled thinking of how these men had locked these girls in there. His blood ran hot through his veins as the anger in him rose.

Nick leveled the rifle to his shoulder and moved through the door into the office. As soon as he passed he could see three men huddled behind two different cars. All of them firing at the front entrance. Nick raised the rifle to eye level and swept right until the first gunman appeared. He squeezed twice and the man dropped. Then he moved an inch farther and squeezed three more times. The next man shouted then fell to the ground. The third gunman turned his weapon toward Nick, but he was too late. Nick had come through at the perfect time and caught all three of them off guard. These men had no idea how to make a stand. Not one of them had thought to watch the back just in case. And it cost them all the rest of their putrid lives.

"Clear!" Nick yelled to Allen.

"All clear . . ." Allen responded. "Gotta be honest. Wasn't sure you were coming."

Nick uncloaked and walked forward into the garage as Allen walked over to him. "Come on. You know better than that."

"Just sayin', thought maybe you'd lost a step."

Nick and Allen walked over to the dead gunmen. Nick had to see for himself. He bent down and went through the khaki pants pockets of the first man. Sure enough, there was a mini frequency jammer. Allen did the same to the second man and no surprise to either of them, he had a jammer as well. Nick knew he had to get to the bottom of who sold him out, and who they sold him out to, or it wasn't going to end well for him.

Now that the building was quiet, they both heard banging and screaming coming from the warehouse in the back. Allen swung his rifle in that direction.

"The hell was that?"

Nick reached out and manually lowered Allen's rifle. "The reason all of these men were shooting at you."

Nick walked forward and Allen fell in behind him. Nick's palms began to fill with sweat, and he was getting a bad taste in his mouth. He wasn't sure what he was going to find inside these trailers. He just hoped none of these poor girls were dead.

13

The banging against the trailer walls, the screaming for help, and the sobbing from the girls trapped inside the trailer were echoing throughout the warehouse. Nick walked up to the back of the first trailer and placed both hands on the latch. He looked at Allen and took a deep breath. He and Allen had been apart of rescue missions like this before. But that was easier to compartmentalize for whatever reason, because it wasn't something happening on his own soil. It was always in a war torn country where vile acts like this were much more expected. Never in Nick's life did he think he would find himself facing this sort of evil on his own soil.

Allen gave his friend a nod, letting him know that whatever they found, they were in this thing together. Nick gave the latch a yank upward and all the horrifying sounds from inside came to a stop. Allen pulled at the doors frame and the two of them pushed it open to the right.

"Reefer trailer," Allen banged the inside wall.

"What?"

Saint Nick 2

"Refrigerated. You can tell by the insulated walls." Allen shrugged. "My brother was a driver."

That's when the smell hit them. These bastards hadn't even let the girls out to use the restroom. Because the lights weren't on in the warehouse, a dark shadow was cast on the back half of the trailer. Nick and Allen saw nothing but black. Then they heard sniffles. They heard quivering fright coming from the darkness. The girls were scared to death.

"It's okay," Nick said softly. "We're here to take you away from all this. You're safe now."

Nick heard what sounded like footsteps moving across the trailer. Slow at first, then all of the sudden, they turned into a run. Out of the shadows came a young woman, maybe thirteen, her hair bouncing in a ponytail above her red hooded sweatshirt. She didn't slow down when she got close to Nick. Instead, she opened her arms and leapt into his. As he wrapped his arms around her and gave her a squeeze, something snapped inside Nick. He'd never been fond of kids. He'd always thought them spoiled brats. But he'd also never seen one be so vulnerable and innocent, and this poor girl instantly changed him forever.

As he held the girl in his arms, he watched in front of him as several more young women emerged from the shadow. He choked back emotion as he was overwhelmed by the moment. He couldn't believe what he was seeing. He couldn't believe adults would actually put these innocent beings in these sorts of conditions, with intent to do even worse to them once they left this warehouse.

The rest of the girls gathered around and what looked like the oldest helped take the girl from Nick's arms to console her.

"Are you really here to help us?" the dark-haired girl asked.

"Yes. We're going to get you out of here," Nick said.

"What about the others?"

Nick's stomach dropped.

"Did you save them too? Please tell me you did." she asked. For the first time, she was showing emotion. A tear ran down her cheek.

"What others?"

"I tried to stop them, but I couldn't. Some time last night, they took six of us out of here. They took my little sister!"

"No, we didn't save them. We just now found out you were here." Nick put his hands on his hips. "But I promise you, we're going to find them."

The other girls gathered around the oldest and comforted her. A new emotion dripped into Nick's veins. Anger. It is was spreading all through him like a cancer.

"We need to get them out of here, Nick," Allen said.

Nick moved forward without conscious thought and took the dark-haired girl by the shoulders.

"What's your name sweetheart?"

"Madison."

"Madison, I promise I'm going to bring your sister home safe. You hear me?"

Madison nodded, but Nick could see there was more.

"What is it?"

"Nick?"

Nick nodded.

"Nick, we don't have a home. None of us. That's how they are able to grab us. We try to find shelters but they do horrible things sometimes too."

Nick couldn't take it any longer. He wasn't used to these sorts of feelings, especially not a full on garbage dump full of them. He pulled out his key fob and pressed to call over the reindeer.

Saint Nick 2

"Well my wife loves kids, so for now she will make sure you're fed and all cleaned up. Sound good?"

A look of hope formed on the eight faces that stared back at him. Nick turned and jumped down out of the trailer. He changed the subject because he just couldn't handle any more.

"I know it's been tough on you girls, but you're going to like what I have to show you."

Nick watched as Allen's face lit up as well. His friend had a big family so Nick knew Allen was affected by seeing these girls this way too. But Allen knew what Nick was about to show the girls and he knew they were going to love it.

They helped the girls down out of the trailer and to the back of the building. Nick and Allen did a sweep of the perimeter, then they locked the two men claiming to just be drug dealers in the back of the van to ensure the safety of the girls.

"They're just on the other side of the van, Nick, " Zeke's voice came through the key fob.

Nick looked over in the direction Zeke was talking about and saw nothing but the end of a gravel parking lot and a cluster of trees. It still amazed him how the cloak worked so well, and there was absolutely no sign of the reindeer and his Humvee sleigh.

"Zeke, alert local authorities about this place. We're on our way home. Is Brooke there?"

"Sure, hold on."

Brooke came through the fob. "I've got some news about Jim and how he might have made his money."

"Good. Can it wait? We just took some girls out of the back of a trailer."

"Oh God! I had to step away for a call. I didn't see you walk them outside!"

"It's okay," Nick used a soft tone. "They're okay. The one's that were left here at least. But they are scared and one of the girl's sister was moved with five others to a different location."

"Oh, that's not good." Brooke was worried. She knew what the next step likely was for these girls.

"Well listen, can you and some of the elves fix up a place for them? Make them feel some comfort?"

"You can't take them back to their families?"

"No Brooke. They informed me they don't have families. Or a home. That's why they were targeted."

"Disgusting. You're going to get the people responsible for this, right?"

"Can you just make up a place for them?"

Nick could hear Brooke choking back emotion. "Of course. They will love it here."

"I have to go. See you soon."

Allen was leading the girls out the back door of the building. Nick tried to summons some of the jolly that the man who handed him these odd abilities would certainly have had. It was like pulling a splinter from beneath a fingernail. It just wasn't natural for Nick.

"Come over here girls. You ready for the ride of your life?"

They all looked up at him—confused.

Nick did his best to play it up for them. "You asked me who I was ... well ... I'm Santa Claus."

Nothing.

Santa wasn't as big of a hit for kids outside the wealthy suburban areas he supposed. These girls probably hadn't seen a Christmas present in years. Or maybe ever. So it was time to take the focus off of himself and put it where it belonged. He raised the key fob.

"And these, are my reindeer."

Nick uncloaked the reindeer and the Humvee sleigh and finally got the reaction he'd hoped for. Every last one of the girls' jaws nearly bounced off the ground.

"But, you're—you're not fat," one of the girls said.

Nick smiled and gave her a wink. "Ms. Claus has me on a diet."

"Is this for real?"

"Go on. You can pet them. Just watch Blitzen, he likes to nibble."

The girls ran forward. If he couldn't give them anything else, at least he gave them a smile.

"I'll grab the sack," Allen said as he started to jog for the ruined rental car.

Nick nodded. Then he watched the girl who's sister was taken from her. Madison had faded to the back of the pack, clearly her mind was with her sibling. The happy feeling Nick got seeing the girls' smile faded like a pair of acid wash jeans. A growing anger replaced it. As soon as he got these girls safely back to the North Pole, he was going to go on a rampage. And every last person who was even the tiniest bit involved with the plot to enslave these girls, and any other child was going to pay.

All of them.

14

The ride back to the North Pole was as fantastical a journey as ever. For everyone except Nick, and from what he could tell, it mattered little to Madison as well. Not even the miracle of a childhood dream becoming a reality right before your eyes can move you beyond worry for a missing family member. It made Nick even more furious that the monsters responsible had stolen this moment from Madison too.

Nick went through the motions when they arrived back at the hangar. Brooke was her usual amazing self as she took the girls under her wing, but Nick had barely said hello. He and Allen moved straight to the War Room where Zeke was ready to brief them on the information Brooke had eluded to earlier.

"What do we got, Z? Keep it short."

Zeke punched a few buttons on his laptop then turned it toward Nick. It was a screen full of numbers. It looked like a bank statement.

"I'm not an accountant, summarize it for me."

Zeke first showed Nick the name at the top of the statement. Jim Calipari. Nick's stomach knotted up. Then Zeke scrolled on the pad until the arrow hovered over one number. Then he highlighted it by double clicking. The number was big.

"This is a deposit of fifty thousand dollars," Zeke said.

"Okay. That's a big deposit, but not life altering, buy a Lamborghini, and move to a mansion in Mexico City big."

"Right. One deposit like this is not. But he has received one of these, once a month, since January of this year."

"Son of a bitch," Allen said.

"All right. That's weird. But it doesn't mean shit for what we are dealing with. Tell me this isn't all you've got? Otherwise we've made zero progress."

"Brooke's friend at the FBI—Anna—looked into where the deposit is coming from. This is where it gets interesting."

Nick glanced up at Allen who had inched a little closer to make sure he didn't miss anything.

"The company making the deposits to Jim is a subsidiary of Thrive Mobil."

Zeke stared at Nick like that was supposed to mean something.

"That a cell phone company?" Nick said.

"No, mob-ill, not mob-ile."

Nick looked at Allen for help.

"Like Exxon Mobil?" Allen said.

"Yes. As in oil."

Before Zeke moved on, the conversation with Brooke about the fancy lunch Jim Calipari had with oil tycoon Jack Frost jumped to mind.

"So they actually are connected," Nick said.

"Yep. Brooke was right. Looks like this Jim guy really did sell you out."

On the surface, it was easy to draw that conclusion. But

there was zero reason somebody Nick had never met would ever give two shits enough to pay that much money to know about the new Santa and his bag of tricks.

"Makes no sense," Allen said, beating Nick to it.

"Right?" Nick stood. "What the hell would Frost want with information about me? I have nothing to do with oil and don't rob the rich to give to the poor. I kill terrorists. And the occasional other scumbag who infringes on people's rights to pursue happiness."

For a reason that Nick couldn't fathom, Zeke smiled at him like he'd won a prize.

"The hell you smilin' about?"

"I thought the same as you at first. Makes no sense. But then I began studying Frost and his story. It's a great one by the way, but the best part was the article in his local newspaper from when Frost was a kid. Apparently his dad was the town hero. Big strong fireman, always saving the day, until the night Frost lost his legs. Apparently Mr. Hero Dad was also a raging alcoholic. He went nuts one night and killed Frost's sister and his mom right in front of him. It was a frozen night, some twenty inches of snow. Frost hit his dad with a bat to try and stop him and his dad went after him. Chased him half a mile into the woods with a blow torch. Kid you not."

"How'd he get away?" Allen said.

"Found a bear trap by a tree and lured his dad over to it. Caught him in it then covered his old man in snow and ice. Froze to death. Unfortunately for Frost he didn't make it back to the house. They found him lying in the snow half frozen himself. Frostbite ate up his legs."

"You're full of it," Nick scoffed. "Frostbite took Jack Frost's legs? Come on."

"I did the same thing!" Zeke said. "But that's why he has

Saint Nick 2

the name Frost. Used to be Jacobs. Everyone called him Frost so much he decided to change it on the count he was also trying to distance himself from his family's horrible past. A follow-up interview with the same paper years later asked him why he ultimately changed his name to Frost. Get this... He said it was because he always loved comic books, and now he could sound like an actual character."

Something strange came over Nick when Zeke told the last part of that story. Somehow all the stuff that made no sense came together in front of him like finding that elusive jigsaw piece that pulls the entire puzzle together.

Nick paced the room. "Hear me out," he told Allen and Zeke. "So this bored oil tycoon, getting old, and rotting all alone, somehow gets wind of this top secret *hero* that inherits Santa's powers—"

"How would he get wind of that—"

"Just let me talk this out, Allen," Nick stayed with his train of thought. "Rich people have friends everywhere. So say someone in his circle mentions something to him about me. The boy in him that always wanted to be one of the comic book character he reads awakens, and he starts sniffing around. Through whoever told him about me, he learns of Jim, the man who first found out about me and just so happens to hate me. He makes him an offer he can't refuse for all the info known about my gadgets and toys, and boom, you have a little boy's wet dream come true. He gets a shot to take down another hero."

"So, in your little story—brilliant one by the way—this rich comic book lover is the villain?" Allen said.

"Apparently."

"Okay, I could stretch the imagination to that. I mean, we do fly through the space-time continuum being pulled by reindeer. *But.* What does all this have to do with trafficking

American girls to Mexico? There's an awfully big leap there."

"I don't know, Allen. There are lots of sickos in this world. Maybe this old rich guy is like this Hollywood pedophile ring everyone knows exists—like with our boy Kevin Swayne—and he just gets off on that sort of thing. Then he figures out it's a way to lure me in?"

"This was my theory exactly after reading up on Frost," Zeke chimed in.

"So fast forward to now," Allen said. "Now what?"

Nick looked at Zeke. "Well?"

Zeke didn't understand. "What?"

"I know you looked Frost up after reading the article and conjuring this sinister tale."

Zeke nodded. "I did."

"Couldn't find him, could you?"

"Not even a trace. He's cloaked himself from the ASE just in case."

"You've got to be kidding me." Allen said. "The old man is jamming our signal?"

"It's him," Nick walked toward the exit. "Which means it's also Jim Calipari. Time to mount up. I'm going to bring Madison's sister home for Christmas. And I'm going to leave a few presents for Jim and his handler along the way."

Allen stopped and shook his head, disappointed. "Cheesiest thing you've ever said, Nick. Do better."

Nick grinned. "Figured it was something a comic book hero would say if he were me."

Allen rolled his eyes as he walked toward Nick. "Just don't do it again."

15

In the suburb neighborhood of Coyoacán, Mexico City, Mexico, the sun was setting on a beautiful estate home that goes back to the time of the Spanish conquest. It once belonged to a captain of the conqueror of Mexico Hernán Cortez Pizarro. It now belonged to Jack Frost. He watched as daylight faded from the cobblestone path in his luscious garden. The sound of the fountain calming the fire within him.

"Señor Frost, your guest has arrived."

Jack turned his wheelchair around to see his butler standing a few feet away.

"Would you like me to assist you?"

"No. Just have him wait for me in the library."

It was Jack's first day at his home in Mexico City. He'd owned it for more than four years. When he bought it he supposed something in the back of his mind was telling him he might need it one day. This was the time. Even though things didn't go well for him at Hector's facility that morning, he felt like he learned a lot about Nick Campos. Even in his mind he couldn't quite call him Santa Claus. It just felt absurd. Though he was fully aware of how hypocritical that was. He was, after all, called Jack Frost.

The last of the sun disappeared so Jack wheeled his way inside. The expansive 13,000 square foot mansion was nice in a lot of ways, but particularly because the space made it easy for him to get around in his chair. He rolled into the living room where Jim was waiting for him. It was time for the next step in setting the trap. Being that it was almost Christmas Eve made it all the more fun. For the first time in his entire life, Jack almost felt festive.

Almost.

"Mr. Frost!" Jim jumped up from the couch at the far wall. He was holding a glass of brown liquid and sporting Tommy Bahama's finest shirt.

"Mr. Calipari. I see you've already helped yourself to the scotch."

"Oh, yeah. Didn't think you'd mind. Sorry."

"It's fine. Just tell me where we are now."

Jim ran his fingers through his sandy-blonde hair and sipped his drink.

"Sure thing. But first I just want to welcome you to Mexico. Gotta say, I love it here more than I thought I would."

"Fine," Jack held up his hand. "Do skip this part. Don't mistake me for your friend."

"Right. Sorry. I've gotten to know a lot of the local police, and even some of the officers at the CNI—the intelligence agency. Great guys. I've put together a team of six people who all have formal training. Now, it's not US training by any means, but they know how to handle themselves and their weapons. More importantly, they are fine working with Hector's men."

"Good. Security is how we will stay in business. Now,

how about the business? How's the contact building going?" Jack said.

"Um, you mean the buyers?"

"Yes."

"Growing list. We've made several deals already and word is spreading in the right circles."

"Good."

Jim ran his fingers through his hair again. Jack could tell it was his nervous tick.

"Uh, about the thing we discussed last week. Look, I'm really putting my neck out here and just want to make sure I'm covered. I never thought I'd be doing this sort of thing, you know?"

"Your next deposit will double. And if you bring me Nick Campos and his reindeer, I'll double it again."

Jim's eyebrows raised. "Double my pay to take out someone I already hate? No problem. I'll mount Rudolph on your wall over there if you want."

"Is there really a Rudolph?"

"I—um, you know, I'm really not sure. He never said anything about it."

"All right then. Walk me through it," Jack said.

"Of course. Walk with me—shit, sorry. Follow me."

Jack couldn't believe this was the man he had to work with. But even though he seemed outwardly to be such a goof, he was really good at what he did. The FBI had taught him well. Jim pulled out an iPad and turned it on.

"Now, because I'm not invisible, I'll have to show you this on the iPad. This is going to blow your mind."

Jim opened an app and handed the iPad to Jack. The screen showed the both of them in the room, but they were colored because it was showing them as heat. The cameras installed were infrared.

"Okay, so the cameras show infrared. Not exactly ground breaking. Hopefully my million dollars extends further than this."

Jim nodded with a wry smile. "Oh yes. Now, watch this." Jim walked over to the library door and shut it. Then over to the light switch on the wall. "Press that green button in the top right hand corner of the screen."

"It turned red, but nothing else happened."

Jim turned off the light. Other than the iPad screen, the room was pitch black. He couldn't see Jim at all.

"You ready for this?" Jim said. He sounded proud.

"Just show me what you've done, all right?"

"Right. Now, press the red button and make it green again. Then you can shut the iPad off and just look at me."

Jack did as Jim asked, expecting very little after what had happened so far. But when he hit the button and made it green, shut off the screen and looked up, he couldn't believe what he saw.

"Huh? Pretty amazing right?"

It was amazing. Jack was looking at Jim, but Jim looked as though he was on fire. The lights in the room were still off. It was as dark as a cave. But Jim was bright red with different shades of yellow and orange at the edges of his body. Jack could see in infrared, without having to wear goggles.

"Is this setup through the entire home?"

"Every room," Jim said. He walked closer to Jack and Jack couldn't help but rub his eyes to make sure it was real. "You can walk through this entire mansion, and everywhere on the grounds outside, and you'll be able to see anything with a heat index."

"It's mesmerizing." Jack looked down and he was aglow himself. A ball of rolling fire.

Saint Nick 2

Jack was truly impressed.

"Won't be any invisible Santa Claus sneaking up on you making sure you're asleep. Not now," Jim said.

Jack enjoyed the fact that he could roam freely and still feel as though he was safe. At least until he was able to rid the world of Santa. But there was one thing that was still missing.

"That's great, but if these special cameras are always on, and I can see anyone with a heat index, they can also see me. So it doesn't exactly help all that much."

"I was hoping you were going to say that." Jim walked closer to Jack and picked up the iPad. "Check this out."

But Jack didn't actually have to take the iPad from Jim. He could tell by looking at his own outstretched arms—or lack there of in the dark room—what Jim had done. The fiery red was gone from Jack's own body. He no longer was being lit up by the infrared sensors. But Jim, he was still ablaze with bright colorful light.

"How is this possible?"

"Remember last week when I had you send me DNA samples of hair, skin, saliva, and blood? Well, the computer system knows it's you sitting in that chair. And it knows not to read you. All with one flip of a switch. It's been programmed to read you like you aren't there. Colder than a refrigerator, which won't even show up if someone is wearing infrared goggles. You would blend right in." Jim paused to laugh. "Which I thought was appropriate because of your name and all."

It was brilliant. Now he could be the invisible one.

"And I know what you're going to ask next," Jim said as he walked over and flipped the light.

Jack tuned his mind back from thinking about the

congruence of his name—Frost—and being invisible due to reading cold in the cameras.

"Even if the power goes out, I had this entire system wired to a generator. You'll be good to go for a couple days in the dark. Or at least until morning."

"Excellent. And security?"

"Two men in the guest house tonight. Two in the van across the street who will intermittently change shifts with the two walking the grounds. All combat trained. And yes, all of their DNA has been entered into the system as well. They too will be invisible in the dark."

"You've done very well, Jim. Money well spent I'd say."

"Thank you. Been doing this side of things for years."

"Will you be close by?" Jack said as he rolled out of the library and down the hall to see Jim out.

"My place is right down the street. Just like you wanted."

"Good. And lastly, how is our little trap coming along?"

"I'd say we're right on target, but I'll know more very soon."

Jack opened the front door and rolled back to let Jim pass. "I want every update as soon as you have it. Including when the girls will be moved."

"Yes sir. Got two going tonight. I'll keep you posted."

16

Nick and Zeke were putting the finishing touches on getting everything ready to go for their ride down to Mexico. They'd loaded up the weapons closet with everything from infrared goggles to belt fed M249 machine guns. That way if they needed to reach inside Santa's sack, help would be waiting there. Long story short: They were ready for a war. As they were busy with all of that, Brooke had gotten the girls all cleaned up, complete with fresh new clothes and the finest of snow boots. She'd shown them around the village and they ended up back in Brooke and Nick's kitchen, baking cookies with Ms. Claus and some elves.

Meanwhile, Zeke had been hard at work digging up anything he could on the exact whereabouts of Jim Calipari and Jack Frost. He'd said it was almost too easy. Flight logs from Los Angeles to Mexico City on Frost's private jet stuck out like a sore thumb. Zeke was following CC footage around the city to determine where Frost had gone once he landed. As Zeke did that, Nick's head elf, Jack, was getting the reindeer fed and loading up the Humvee sleigh.

At this point, Nick had been on enough missions that all of this had become second nature to his helpers at the NP. But the stakes, on a personal level, were palpably higher for everyone involved. The workers at the North Pole were used to doing things for children, but they weren't used to saving their lives by extracting them from very bad people. Nick was impressed by how highly motivated they all were to make this thing a success. Nick just hoped he could come through in the end.

The stakes were higher for him as well. When he kissed Brooke goodbye, Madison charged him before he could get to the door and threw her arms around him.

"Please save my sister," she'd said. Tears running down her cheeks. "I'll do anything. You can give my presents to everyone else for the rest of my life. Just please bring her back to me. She's all I've got. And I know she must be so scared."

Nick didn't have any words. Thankfully, Brooke hurried over and promised Madison that Nick would do everything he could to bring her sister home. Nick just nodded and walked out the door. If he'd stayed in there any longer he might have lost it. And that wasn't a feeling he was used to. He didn't like it either. It added stress and pressure to an already nearly impossible situation. Brooke could see that, that's why she stepped in. He was grateful to have a wife that knew him so well.

Now it was time for him and Allen to put full focus on the task at hand. Everything was setup for success. Almost too much so for Nick's liking. Something about how easy it was to find out that Frost had flown to Mexico wasn't sitting well with him. He wasn't going to walk into a trap for a third time, but he still had to walk in. There was just no way around that. And if Jack Frost and all his minions were

Saint Nick 2

ready and waiting as Nick suspected they might be, Nick and Allen had to be prepared to take them all head on.

The two of them hopped up in the Humvee. From the looks of the inside, they weren't ready for war at all, but more like a picnic. Since Nick had already loaded up the weapon room, they only needed the sack for their weapons. No sense junking up the car when you can just have the one "empty" bag. However, Jack had provided them with provisions in case the job ran longer than expected. So it was snacks and water in the sleigh instead of weapons and ammo.

Nick put the Humvee in neutral when he noticed a folded piece of paper sitting on the dash. "Santa" was written on the front in ink. It wasn't Brooke's handwriting, he could tell that immediately because the penmanship was much too neat.

"What's that?" Allen said.

"You read it," Nick picked up the note and tossed it to Allen.

"It's for Santa. You should read it. Besides, what if it's from Brooke and there's a naked picture inside."

Nick looked over at his friend and laughed. "If you thought that was a possibility you would have already torn that note open."

Allen laughed. "Touché." Then he unfolded the note. "Looks like a kid's writing. You sure you—"

"Just read the damn note so we can get out of here."

"They're just feelings, Nick," Allen morphed his voice to sound like a therapist. "Everyone has them. Even a big, strong man like you. Just let them out. It's cathartic."

"Like you even know what the hell cathartic means."

"What does it mean?" Allen laughed.

"Hell if I know."

Allen had effectively lightened the mood. For that, Nick was grateful.

"All right. It says: Dear Santa, it's Madison, but I guess you already knew that." Allen paused and looked over at Nick to see if he did already know that.

Nick shrugged and shook his head.

Allen continued with Madison's note. *Emmy and me have never had a whole lot in our lives. Our parents were junkies, so we didn't live with them very long. We've bounced around a lot since then. Foster care and other places. Some of the foster parents were good, some just wanted us for the paycheck. One of them I had to get me and Emmy escaped from because when the man would drink too much he'd either get mad at everyone, or want to touch us.*

I'm sorry, I don't know why I'm telling you all this. You already know it. I guess I'm just trying to say that even though things have been hard for Emmy and me, and we ain't had nothin, I always knew it was going to be okay, because we always had each other. Now I'm real scared that might not be again either. So I guess like some silly movie on TV, I'm asking for a Christmas miracle. I didn't have any hope as I sat in the back of that trailer after they took her. Not until I saw you and that funny looking guy with the cool beard open up that trailer door. I know you ain't God, Santa. But I know you're real good at giving people what they want for Christmas, and all I want is my sister. Nothing else for the rest of my life.

And I know you don't need it, cause you see everything, but I put the only picture I've got of my sister in your cupholder. Just so you know for sure who to grab if you see her.

Thank you for trying to help me. No one else ever has. And no matter if you bring her back or not, I love you for trying for me. Your friend, Madison.

Allen let his arms fall into his lap and hung his head

with a sigh. It was a heavy moment. Nick was entirely unprepared for it emotionally. He'd never dealt with anything like this, and had no idea that a kid he didn't even know could make him feel so much. Though all he wanted to do was move out and go fight, his hand reached for the cupholder and picked up the picture.

Emmy was a beautiful blonde-haired little girl with ocean blue eyes. Her smile was as bright as a neon light. Nick flipped the picture over and scribbled on the back was *Emmy Jacobs - 9yrs old*. A long exhale left Nick's lungs.

"Well my friend . . ." Allen folded the note and placed it back on the dash. "No pressure," he said sarcastically. Then he gave Nick a hard pat on the chest.

Nick looked his friend in the eye. "I'm going to bring that little girl back to her sister, Allen. I don't care if I have to burn Mexico City down."

"Then we'd better get movin'. I do my best work at night."

17

By the time Nick shot through the wormhole with Allen and the reindeer, Zeke had pinpointed Jack Frost's position in Mexico City. Jack was still using a jammer to keep off the ASE's radar, but Nick knew that was just posturing by that point. A man like Frost isn't stupid. If he's clever enough to jam the ASE's signal, he's smart enough to know that Nick would easily be able to track Frost's movements the old school way by flight logs and old fashioned CC cameras.

So the question then was, why was frost "luring" Nick to him? What did he want? Clearly he has some role in the human trafficking ring, that is why he'd had Hector Ramirez try and trap him. Nick might think it was just to keep from being caught by Nick, but this plan of Frost's had clearly been in motion long before Nick knew anything about Ramirez and the Atlanta trafficking ring. Did that mean Nick was right with what he said in the War Room? Was this about a wealthy man so disconnected from reality that he wanted to live out his comic book fantasies by having an archenemy? As absurd as that sounded, Nick did just zip in from the North Pole in less than sixty seconds being pulled by flying reindeer.

Nick circled the neighborhood on the outskirts of the city where Frost's mansion was situated. Apparently he'd bought a relic of a house so the floor plans and plenty of pictures of every inch of the place were all online. Zeke had sent over a few files that Allen was looking over while Nick found a place to sit the Humvee sleigh down. Allen would know every inch of that place in a matter of minutes. Even though Frost was obviously going to have a heavy load of security at the estate, with the information that Nick and Allen now had about what they were walking into, and their skills as elite combat veterans, it wouldn't matter if Frost had a small army.

Nick didn't want to jinx things, but it was essentially suicide for Frost. The only thing that worried Nick was that he wouldn't be able to find out where the girls were being kept in all the fray. And that was a major concern.

Nick spoke through his mic letting the reindeer know where to bring the sleigh to the ground. This part was easy as well because the mansion Frost purchased overlooked a hundred acre National Park. Plenty of space, and tree coverage for Nick to let the reindeer stay while he and Allen did their work.

As they broke through the atmosphere, Nick could see that it was a clear night. The stars were shining all around him. The reindeer pulled them along the bed of city lights below, shining even brighter than the lights from above. They wound around above the streets, cloaked in Santa's invisible magic, then pulled forward as the dark National Park came into view. The reindeer coasted to the ground and came to a stop at the foot of a tree-filled hill. Jack's place was supposedly just on the other side of the climb.

"Here we are," Nick said.

Allen leaned over the middle console with an iPad and pictures of the estate were pulled up. Allen began scrolling through, pointing out potential entry points, weak spots, and places he felt they should avoid. Nick studied with fervor. He wanted to be able to navigate the place in the dark as if he'd been there before. Something not easy to do with such a large estate, but it was workable. Both he and Allen had been through worse.

The grounds were expansive for an estate in the city. Almost three acres. The guesthouse at the back of the property would be their first stop. Once they cleared it they could methodically work toward the home. This would normally prove to be the most difficult part to enter and remain undetected, but Nick knew there would be security everywhere inside, so staying quiet wasn't really his intent. It was not being seen while they were inside that mattered. Which at that point, he knew the cloaking device would be useless. That's why he'd come prepared.

One of the first things he and Zeke spoke about when Nick and Allen made it back from Atlanta with their lives, was how to keep that from happening again. Zeke worked all through the night, and with the help of the best workers known to man, he and the elves had two new suits, custom fitted for Nick and Allen. Their sole purpose was to ensure that when someone was clever enough to use infrared to work around Nick's cloaking device, they would still be invisible.

Nick thought the quick work Zeke and the elves had done in the workshop was genius. All of them, however, had

Saint Nick 2

insisted it was easy. They went into the technicalities of how the suits Nick and Allen were currently wearing kept them invisible to infrared, but all Nick cared about was that they worked. Seeing was believing and when they showed Nick the infrared camera after he'd put on the suit, he had to unzip it and pull it down a bit to prove it wasn't a trick. When he did, his exposed chest glowed red. The rest of him? It blended in with the cool surroundings of the room. The long and short of it was that Zeke had essentially constructed the suits to make Nick and Allen like cold-blooded reptiles. Snakes don't show up on infrared because their blood isn't hot enough to render. The suit's *skin* did the same by masking their body heat with an outer shell that stayed cooler than the room.

"We really have to wear these masks?" Allen said.

"You saw how good they worked," Nick said. "But you can look like a floating head up there if you want. Just know your head is so big it's an easy target."

The two of them got out of the Humvee and walked around to the back.

"I look like Spiderman on steroids," Allen said.

Nick stretched the crotch of his suit as much as he could as he hit the button on the lift gate. "They really do hug. But I like it better than the alternative."

"I'm not saying I don't, Nick. But we look ridiculous."

Nick shrugged and pulled his mask down over his face. It was pitch black until he pressed the button by his ear, then the two cameras for eyes came on. It was amazing. The eyes had to stay covered to conceal their body heat, so Zeke attached two cameras with small monitors wrapping around their eyes like virtual reality goggles. Zeke just called them reality goggles. The amazing part was that they were wide angled lenses and they could actually see better than with the naked eye. Nick could also toggle between night-vision and regular with two taps on the same button that turned the cameras on.

"We have got to share all of this tech with the military Nick. This will keep our soldiers so much safer."

"Once we prove they work, it's the next thing on Santa's delivery list."

Nick and Allen bumped fists, then pulled two suppressed M4 Carbines from the sack and strapped them around their shoulders. Then took out two suppressed Berettas as their sidearms. Though Nick hoped the Beretta would be the only weapon he needed, they had to be prepared for worse. Finally, they pulled a couple of tactical belts with spare M4 and Beretta magazines already equipped, strapped them around their waists and shut the Humvee's gate.

"Let's go cut the head off of this trafficking snake and get those girls back to safety," Allen said.

"No splitting up. If we work together we can face anything they throw at us up there."

Allen nodded and began walking to the foot of the hill.

Nick pressed the button over his right ear, opening communication with the War Room. "Zeke, you with me?"

"We're here."

"*We're* here?"

"Hey Nick," Brooke said.

"Well isn't that a song in my ear."

"I'm here with you. The girls are in good hands, I couldn't miss this. We've got your six."

"Better words were never spoken. How's it looking up there?"

"Just as you would suspect. Quiet. Except there is also no power on at the estate either. Nothing."

"What?"

"They're ready for you guys, Nick."

Nick swung the M4 around into his hands. "No they're not."

18

Nick and Allen began their wooded ascent toward Frost's estate. Both of them had switched to night vision because without it, they couldn't see five feet in front of them in those trees.

"Everything is quiet," Brooke said in Nick's ear.

Too quiet, Nick thought.

"Other lights on in the neighborhood?" Nick whispered.

"Yes," Brooke said. "This is not an outage, or an accident."

The two of them approached the top of the hill.

"Going silent," Nick said. "Only talk to me if you have to."

"No mercy, sweetheart. These people sell children to the highest bidder."

Nick didn't need the extra motivation, but the shot of adrenaline that hit him after Brooke's words was a welcome addition to his heightened senses. As he and Allen weaved around trees, the grounds at the back of the estate came into view in the green hue of the built-in night-vision lenses in their masks. Nick toggled the night-vision off for a moment to take in just how dark it was. There was just a small amount of glow from the stars, but not enough to pick up movement. He toggled back to night-vision.

Nick was hot inside his special suit. It felt like a diving suit the way it hugged him and trapped in the heat. It amazed him that it was able to hold all that in and remain unseen by infrared. The landscape was open in front of him. The clearing continued for an acre or more to his right, and about the same on his left. The only difference was that on the left, there was a small building. Nick motioned to Allen with his hand by waving to him that they would start there.

Nick took the lead and pushed to the trees' edge. He exchanged his M4 for the Beretta on his hip. Though both were suppressed, the Beretta would be the quieter of the two. He could see that the building in front of him was some sort of maid or service quarters. Looked like just enough room to be the size of a one bedroom apartment. Nick checked his surroundings, and when he saw nothing, he jogged forward and put his back against the stucco wall. There was a window right beside him, then the door after that. He pushed his ear close to the window seal but couldn't hear anything.

Then both he and Allen heard something snap behind them. It sounded like a tree branch. They both swung their weapons around and pointed them in that direction. Then Nick swung back the opposite way to keep an eye on all sides. It was quiet on top of that hill. Street noise was non existent, and other than the occasional plane flying over and noise from local critters, there wasn't much going on. That's why the snapping sound so easily got their attention.

Nick felt Allen pat him on the back. Nick turned and Allen motioned he was going to have a look. Nick shook his head and waved him off. He didn't want to separate. Night vision would not allow Nick to decipher Allen from the enemy. He wasn't about to lose Allen to friendly fire, or vice versa. Instead, Nick put two fingers up to his eyes, telling him just to keep an eye out. Nick watched him nod.

It was time to make some progress. Nick ducked below the window and moved toward the door. He reached for the handle but pulled back when he saw it start to move. Then he heard the muffled baritone of a man's voice on the other side of the wall. That meant unless this man was on the phone or on a COM system, there are two men inside.

The door cracked open and Nick took advantage. He slid forward with a front kick to the bottom of the door. When it swung inward he rushed forward and shot the man inside twice in the gut. As he groaned in pain, Nick jumped for the shadow in his peripheral. He grabbed for whatever he could and managed the sleeve of a shirt. He felt a rifle knock against his right arm as it dangled from the man's shoulder. It was loose, meaning Nick wasn't in danger of being shot, so instead of reaching for the gun, he twisted his hips and threw a short uppercut in the direction of the man's chin. He only half connected, but it was enough to throw the man off balance and Nick wrapped his arms around him beneath his ass, picked him up, and drove him down onto the ground.

When Nick landed on top of him he shoved his forearm into the man's neck and applied pressure. "Talk to me or you're dead. There is no other way."

Nick let off the pressure for a response. He heard Allen move in behind him. The man said something in Spanish. Nick got Allen's attention to come and translate. Allen moved in, traded Nick positions, and Nick went back to the door to make sure no one was sneaking up on them. For the moment it was clear. He heard Allen whispering with the man so Nick took the time to check in.

"What are you seeing," Nick whispered as he radioed the War Room. As he spoke he went to check on the man he shot. He was dead. The man's pockets produced yet another frequency jammer. That's why the ASE was continually being tricked. Zeke was going to have to find a way to work around that.

"Nothing has changed, Nick," Brooke said.

"Find us a way in."

"We've been over this, Nick. As much as you don't want to hear it, it's the chimney if you want to stay quiet."

"I'm not going down the chimney."

"Why? Don't be stubborn, Nick. If you're cliché enough to fly on a sleigh pulled by reindeer, what's the difference in going down the chimney? You'd do it if you were on assignment somewhere and none of this Santa stuff ever happened. You know you would. Don't let your ego cloud your judgement."

Brooke was right. He didn't know why he was having the mental block of refusing to go down a chimney. Especially if it gave them a tactical advantage. There were very few double-wide chimney's in residential homes. Mostly they were installed in hotels that had large lobbies. She was right, he would be a fool not to take advantage.

"Let me know when you see movement," Nick said as he clicked off the COM.

Nick turned back to Allen in time to watch him deliver a punch to the gut. The man coughed from the blow and Allen covered his mouth. That's when they heard the static. Nick rushed forward and picked up the man's arm. He was holding a two-way radio. The static was him releasing the button. Whoever was on the other end now knew Nick and Allen were there.

"Time to move," Nick said to Allen. "If they weren't already on high alert, they are now."

"Let's just blow the place up," Allen whispered. "Forget this tactical shit. They're all bad."

"What if the girls are being held inside?"

Allen didn't respond to that. He moved on, "We really going down the chimney?"

"I'm open to better ideas."

"I've got none."

"Chimney it is," Nick said. "At least it's on brand."

"Ho ho ho," Allen said, stealing Nick's thunder.

19

Nick decided it was easiest just to unhook the Humvee and take the Sleigh to the roof. That would also give them the chance to grab the repelling gear since he couldn't actually just jump down the chimney and be okay. His head elf, Jack, swears the fat man could do it, but doesn't have any proof, or any idea how. Nick knew that by the time he and Allen made it on top of the roof, Frost's men will have rallied inside the house, ready for a fight. There was no way to avoid it. Without knowing if the girls were in that house, Nick was forced to take the delicate approach and sneak his way inside.

The reindeer dropped down out of the sky and landed soft as a fifteen hundred thread count sheet on top of the roof. Allen fixed the grappling hook to the chimney and slowly lowered the rope. Nick climbed in first. He wanted to say something clever, but he was too focused on the coming close-quarter fire fight that was about to ensue. He cloaked himself and began lowering down the small brick tunnel. There was plenty of room on both sides of him. He'd been in tighter spots many times as a Ranger.

About halfway down he felt the rope pull. When he looked up he saw the bottom of Allen's boots. Zeke said he'd tested the suits they were wearing under all conditions, and supposedly now that infrared wouldn't be able to see them, he was back to being invisible. Something that would probably mean the difference between life or death in a short minute. He trusted Zeke, but Zeke's level of perfectionism wasn't quite up to par with Nick's yet. But it was getting there.

Nick looked down and saw the floor just below him. He slowed his pace and landed on his tip-toes. He didn't move a muscle until he could help lower Allen in place. He was able to keep him from knocking over the wood in the middle of their landing area. Once they were both down, Nick took a deep breath. The heat in the anti-infrared suit was a problem. He could feel the sweat building. However, there was no time to worry about comfort, the girls this man was selling certainly couldn't.

It was total darkness where Nick and Allen stood. Nick crouched and had a look around. He was in what he would call the living room. It was massive, and not a lot of clutter around in the way of furniture. He was about to raise up and give the okay to move when a shadow passed out in front of him in the hallway. Then another right behind it. They were both moving fast. Nick assumed the suspense of when he and Allen would storm the castle was beginning to get to them.

Nick tapped on Allen leg then eased out of the fireplace. The half of the room that lead to the right was clear so he moved in that direction. He stayed low with his Beretta out in front. He made it behind a large dining table and stopped. There was an open doorway that looked like it lead to a hallway. They were at the back of the house. The only sounds

Saint Nick 2

he could hear was a little commotion in the direction that he saw the shadows moving toward. He felt Allen on his hip so he turned to move on. Just then someone walked right up to the back door that led out to the lanai.

Nick was close enough to the man in the hallway that he could see he wasn't wearing goggles. This surprised Nick, but he couldn't dwell on it. The wrong move here could start a firefight. And though he liked his and Allen's chances, anything can happened when bullets start flying.

Just then the floor creaked behind them in the direction of the fireplace. Nick didn't look he just moved left, deeper behind the dining table. He peeked up and over and a man was moving slowly their way. Allen sucked himself behind a chair on the other side. They were in danger of being trapped, and he did not like the position they were in as a good place to make a stand.

The man coming from the fireplace whispered something in Spanish.

"No," the man by the back door answered.

Then both of them walked toward each other, stopping right at the end of the dining table.

"The man on the right asked if the other had seen anything," Brooke spoke in his ear via the COM.

Nick jumped when he heard her voice, but was happy to get the translation. Brooke studied Spanish in college and early in her law enforcement career she was used a lot as a translator. And Brooke never thought he listened when she told her stories.

"Do you think the camera system is working?" Brooke continued to interpret. "Because I haven't seen any infrared."

The suits were working.

"Let's just turn the lights on. This is stupid. I'm not afraid of Santa Claus anyway."

Just when Nick was considering jumping the two men, Brooke came back. "Nick, don't make a move yet." She really was in his head. "I'm calling the reindeer away for a minute. Zeke said he put a flash grenade in a slot under the hitch on the sleigh. He said he can just hit a button to drop it. I'm going to have him do right in the garden. Should get a lot of attention. I'll set the reindeer down across the street. The neighbor has a big side yard. That way if you need them, they'll be close. Please be careful. I love you"

Nick looked through the chairs' legs under the table. Allen could hear the conversation in his ear as well. They gave each other a nod. Nick slowly fit his Beretta in his belt holster. Then he pulled gently on the strap around the shoulder till he felt the M4 in his hands. The man in front of him spoke into a radio. And just as Nick posted up on one knee, Brooke came back in his ear.

"He just told someone that he didn't think the infrared camera system is working. We have to do this now. On my mark.

"3 . . ." Brooke counted down. "2 . . . 1 . . ."

It was so dark surrounding the house, and so quiet, that when the flashbang ignited in the garden, the light screamed through the windows of the mansion and the pop seemed to reverberate off the windows. The next few seconds were amateur hour in that house. The two men went running to join the others, and it sounded like every single one of them were shooting blindly into the garden. Nick surged forward, M4 extended, and moved into the room behind them. Allen stayed behind in the hallway to guard Nick's back.

Nick would have felt bad for these men under a different circumstance. Four of them were standing at the door that led to the garden, blindly firing into the night. Driven by

Saint Nick 2

pure fear. But it wasn't different circumstances. These men were aiding a man who was ruining the lives of children. No mercy could be shown.

Nick squeezed the trigger on his rifle. He had his M4 set to three round bursts. He was terrible at math, since the M4 had a thirty-round mag, all he had to do was count to ten. He made it all the way to the third man with three squeezes. They all dropped straight to the ground. The fourth man was able to dive out of sight to his right. Nick went to the ground himself when he heard Allen firing behind him. He swung around in time to see Allen backing into the room. Nick popped up and checked the window but the gunman had been quick to run.

Nick poked his upper body out the garden door but the man had already made it around the corner.

Because the shooting had stopped, the night was still. That's why Nick was able to hear a car start up around the front of the house. All he could think about was Frost getting away, and losing track of the girls who were taken.

He couldn't let either of those two things happen.

20

Allen trailed Nick up the walk path that wrapped around to the front of the mansion from the garden. Nick knew he didn't have to worry about his back, so he focused on what was in front of him, making sure he kept them both safe from his angle. Nick hadn't seen any sign of the gunman who'd just eluded him a moment ago, but he did hear the squeal of tires on pavement as he moved through the tall wooden fence.

In front of him, in the circular driveway, he just watched as the taillights of a low sitting sports car rocketed away from the mansion. The bright red lights on the back almost got him killed. A string of bullets splintered the fence as he dove to the ground. He didn't have to wonder how they saw him. He could see the glow of the taillights lighting him up like a beacon. Fortunately he didn't have to shoot, Allen was coming through the fence and took the man by the driveway down.

"They're on the move," Nick said as he jumped to his feet. "We've gotta go!"

Nick took a sweep with his eyes across the front of the

mansion, but didn't see any more gunman. Then he looked to the neighbors across the street. He obviously couldn't see the reindeer that were supposed to be waiting in the side yard there, but he absolutely noticed the taillights of the get away car lighting up the back end of a van out on the curb.

"Van!" Nick shouted. "My twelve!"

Nick watched Allen swing around and point his rifle toward the van. Nick whistled for the reindeer as loud as he could, but the mesh of his mask kept him from getting anything out. He and Allen moved to their right behind a large stone statue. Nick ripped off his mask but before he could whistle, he was returning fire. The men at the van were firing their way. It sounded like two guns, and they were better shots than their buddies. Bullets were ricocheting off the statue and Nick pulled into himself to try to stay behind it.

These two men had some combat experience, Nick could tell. When they were getting close to the end of their magazines, one stopped firing while the other bled his out. Then he started back up while his friend changed his mag so there was always one gun running on Nick and Allen. It's exactly what Nick would have done.

But they couldn't fire forever. And they knew it. That's why they stopped firing and jumped back in the van. Before Allen could fire his weapon, Nick whistled for the reindeer. Then both he and Allen lit up the front end of the van. Allen switched out his magazine while Nick let off some more three-round bursts. Their gunfire was echoing off the surrounding hills.

While staying alive was as important as anything to getting those girls back safely, Nick knew he also couldn't let that car get too far down the road. If it made it down the winding hills of the neighborhood before Nick could get an arial view with the sleigh, they might lose them long enough to lose those girls. The van continued toward them, easing off the road and onto the end of the driveway. Then it took a sharp turn to where the passenger door was facing Nick and Allen.

Nick did not like the look of that. And he liked it even less when a large spark lit up at the van's window. He didn't have to hear the rocket before he knew what was coming their way.

"Cover!" Nick shouted as he took two quick steps and dove for the ground. Behind him the rocket exploded into the statue. Pieces of stone began raining down on Nick.

Nick whistled again for the reindeer then shouted directions for them as he pointed at the street. "Start down the road! I'll catch up!"

Allen had a fresh magazine locked in so he kept the men in the van from unloading another explosive on them. Since the van's back end was now to the street, Nick knew this was their chance. He slid his hand to his belt as he ejected his empty mag and then replaced it with a fresh one.

"To the street!" Nick shouted to Allen. Then he began firing at the van. He was holding his aim on the passenger door. He couldn't tell what was going on inside. Allen came bounding out of the shrubs and Nick paused his gunfire long enough for Allen to pass in front of him. Nick started firing again with his right hand while he toggled the cloak off on the reindeer and the sleigh. Out of the corner of his eye he could see the lights on their harnesses as they scampered down the road. They had done as he asked. But now he had to get going himself.

"Nick!" Allen shouted.

Allen had caught up to the back of the sleigh and pulled himself on. Nick began to jog as he held fire on the van until

Allen could situate himself in the sleigh. They'd left an M249 belt-fed machine gun laying in the backseat. Nick knew once he heard that monster start roaring he could kick it into high gear and catch the sleigh. He hit the trigger for the tenth time and he was out of rounds. He let the M4 hang from his shoulder strap and pulled his Beretta. But he couldn't keep his eye on everything, and as he was pulling the Beretta from its holster his foot caught on a rock and he went face first into the patch of grass that lay in front of the driveway's pavement. His pistol skidded away from him on the blacktop.

"Whoa!" Allen shouted.

As Nick was picking himself up off the ground a shadow reappeared in the window of the van. He didn't think he could get to his gun in time to defend himself. He was going to curl up into a ball to make himself as small as possible, but he knew from the tactics these gunmen used earlier that they would easily be able to shoot him. And if they were going to shoot him, he wasn't going to go down without a fight.

21

Nick sprang forward and sprinted for his gun. As he ran he tensed up in anticipation of hot bullets melting through his skin. Just as he dove for his gun, the bullets came. But not the ones he was expecting. When he heard what sounded like helicopter propellers cutting through the air, he knew it was the M249 SAW machine gun being held at full throttle. The window at the back of the van exploded and the back door was getting chewed up at an incredible rate.

Allen laying down cover fire gave Nick a window, and he took advantage. He rolled to one knee and squeezed four shots off at the passenger side window.

Then he ran.

The van was taking a hailstorm of damage so the driver hit the gas and tried to turn away. Allen ran out of rounds so Nick shot backward as he ran to try and keep the gunmen from firing at him.

Nick whistled for the reindeer to start moving again. The sleigh edged forward out in front of him. He had about

Saint Nick 2

thirty yards to go. He couldn't worry about shooting anymore, Nick just had to run.

"Asses and elbows, Nick!" Allen shouted.

Nick remembered they'd also put a spare drum beside the M249, and it was apparent when Allen had locked it in, because the tat-tat-tat-tat of the SAW filled the air. Nick kicked it into high gear and the reindeer and the sleigh began sloping down the hill. The sparks from the rattling machine gun told Nick exactly where he needed to get to.

Allen stopped firing. The van had to have been out of commission at that point.

"Trees coming up, Nick! Let's go!"

Nick surged forward and finally caught up to the moving sleigh. Allen leaned over and held out his hand. Nick grabbed it, jumped forward to put one foot on the hitch where the Humvee connects, he hurdled up over the tall back of the sleigh's back seat. He landed on the padded seat, but his momentum carried him down to the floor. Then he was pinned against the bottom of the bench as his stomach dropped when the reindeer pulled upward. There was no gunfire accompanying them off, Allen had wiped the two men on the ground right out.

With no time to celebrate the small win, Nick pulled the key fob from his pocket and pressed the button for the War Room.

"You made it!" Brooke answered.

"Get Zeke on the ASE to find that car!" Nick shouted as the wind swirled through the open sleigh. "I know Frost is in it. If he gets away, we'll lose those girls!"

"Negative," Brooke said. "The ASE is jammed on that car—"

"It can't be! We can't lose it!"

"BUT!" Brooke spoke over him. "Zeke followed it the old

school way by hacking the CC cameras in the neighborhood. But we lost him when he turned left onto G. Pérez Valenzuela."

"What? Is that a road?"

"Yes, a main artery."

"Can you direct me? Put the ASE on us and match it up with GPS if you can. We have to find him!"

"Zeke is on it, just head west for a minute."

Nick looked up into the dark sky.

"Right there," Allen said as he pointed behind them. "North star!"

Nick hopped over the seat into the front. He was going to try to intuit the directions to the reindeer but it was easier for him just to steer them, so he picked up the reins and pulled left. He spun them around until they were headed west.

"Brooke?"

"Hold on, he's into the traffic light cameras. Just wait a second."

"We don't have a second!"

"Nick!" Brooke sounded off.

He took a deep breath and regained his composure. Allen was in the back with the sack, readying the weapons for another showdown. Nick hit the cloak on the reindeer so he wouldn't cause a national disturbance with his UFO and brought them down about fifty feet closer to the ground. The neighborhood and the National Park gave way to city streets below. There were lights everywhere. Nick didn't know how Zeke was going to find the car. But at least he knew its direction, that offered a splash of hope.

"What type of car is it?" Allen shouted over the wind. He had removed his mask.

"Lamborghini Gallardo," Brooke said. Her voice echoed through the sleigh's speaker's now.

Something pinged in Nick's mind. "Lamborghini? Didn't you say that's the car your friend said Jim showed up to lunch driving that day in LA?"

"I thought the same thing, I just didn't want to rattle you," Brooke said.

"Rattle me? If anything, it makes me want to catch him even more!"

"And it makes sense," Allen said. "Frost is handicapped, so he needs someone to drive him."

"Where do you think they're going, Nick?" Brooke said.

Nick had been thinking about this already. "Protection. He's going somewhere where he can put a lot of other people between us and him."

"Sounds safe."

"Sarcasm, Brooke?"

"Just trying to lighten the—hold on, Zeke found him!"

A slow drip of adrenaline leaked into Nick's system.

"Linking the car to your GPS. Steer right!"

Nick did as Brooke said. The reindeer responded to Nick's touch.

"Little more then let it even out."

Nick followed her direction. The sleigh leveled out and the reindeer stretched out in front of him. The city lights beyond that. The lost girls somewhere tucked away inside of all those people and places. Nick sent up a silent prayer that Frost and Jim would lead him right to them. And if they didn't, that he could get the girls' whereabouts out of them before he took their lives.

22

"I lost them," Zeke's muffled voice made it through the sleigh's speakers.

Nick's blood ran cold. "The hell did he just say?"

"What? You're sure?" Brooke asked him.

Nick heard Zeke's voice but couldn't understand what he was saying.

"Damn it, Zeke! Grab a mike and let me hear what you're saying!"

"I said, I was tracking the car camera to camera, then lost them. They must have taken an exit."

"Well find them!"

"Nick, calm down," Brooke said. "He's doing the best he can."

"Well do better!"

"There are hundreds of cameras in the area, Nick. It could take a while, but it's all we can do!"

That wasn't good enough. Nick understood what Zeke was doing was difficult, but so were shootouts in blacked out mansions.

"Circle until we find something, Nick. Don't get too far away from the area you're in now."

"There has to be a quicker way. Come on! Zeke you'd better fix this All Seeing Eye, cause it can't see shit right now. It's worthless!"

"What about the trailer?" Allen said.

Nick jerked his head to the right to look at Allen. "What are you thinking?"

"The trailer we found the girls in. It was a reefer trailer, remember?"

"What?" Nick peeled back to when they opened the trailer and Allen mentioned it was insulated. "Oh, you mean refrigerated. So what? How does that help?"

"It might not. Just—"

"Or it might be their cover." Nick's mind had caught up.

"What are you guys talking about?" Brooke said.

"The trailer we found the girls in was refrigerated. Maybe that's how they get the girls across the border. Load some things in the front of the trailer as a front. There any businesses close that use a lot of refrigeration? Meat company? Frozen food company? Maybe this is their cover for the entire trafficking ring."

"Yeah, but it's not that simple, Nick," Allen said. "Sure, those are popular businesses for reefers, but they also haul things like cosmetics, electronic equipment, and medicine in them to keep them cool. Hell, my brother had a load one time of just some stupid expensive art so the paint wouldn't melt."

"That's it!" Zeke shouted.

Nick and Allen both perked up.

"Remember, Brooke?" Zeke said. "We both laughed about it when we were looking over Jack Frost's holdings how cliché it was for an ultra rich guy to own an art gallery."

"Oh yeah," Brooke said. "And it was in Mexico!"

"Find that address! Fast!" Nick shouted. "Nice work Allen. I knew there was a reason I kept you around."

"You mean it isn't my charming personality? Or how I saved your ass in the gunfight earlier?"

"Got it!" Brooke shouted. "You're close! Looks like a warehouse on Google Maps. Sending it to you now."

Nick's phone dinged. There was no function for a sleigh pulled by reindeer so he had to slow the reindeer to follow the directions like they were in a car. Brooke was right, it wasn't far. They were only a mile away, and didn't have to worry about traffic. Perks.

"They must be inside already, because the ASE is picking up their car," Brooke said. "They are there boys. Go get those girls and bring them home for Christmas. We'll be keeping an eye on you if you need anything."

"Get my bourbon ready darling. We'll be home soon."

Nick put the key fob away and steered the reindeer into the last turn. He dropped them another thirty feet and the warehouse came into view.

"Okay boys and girls," Nick said to the reindeer. "Sit us on top of that building."

Nick turned to find Allen locking in a fresh magazine and putting a spare in his belt. He tossed Nick a spare for his M4 and another mag for his Beretta. Allen picked up his mask and held it up.

"What do you think? We need these?"

"Did we when we hunted terrorists in caves?" Nick smirked.

"No, but you really do look ridiculous with it on. So please wear it? You're like a reject Deadpool with an unimaginative suit."

Saint Nick 2

"I'm telling Zeke you said that. He'll short out your mike if you're not careful."

Nick and Allen removed the earpieces from the masks and inserted them in their ears as the sleigh glided softly down to the roof of the warehouse. A place that was far too big for something as small as dealing fine art. But what did Nick know, he was cultured in the arts about as much as a seven year-old who still eats his boogers.

Nick grabbed the charging handle on the M4, pulled it all the way back and released it. His fresh mag was ready to fire, and so was he. Allen got up to join him and they both stepped down off the sleigh. Nick walked over to the edge where he'd spotted the service ladder on the way in.

"What, no chimney this time?" Allen said.

"Let's make this quick. The longer we stay here the more likely the cavalry gets called in."

Allen nodded and followed Nick down the ladder. There were loading bays to the right and they made their way right over to them. There hadn't been any other cars in the lot other than the very conspicuous white Lamborghini. But that didn't mean there weren't men inside. If there weren't any, then that meant the girls probably weren't there either, and that's the last thing Nick wanted.

Just as the two of them were approaching the first bay, the large garage door jerked and began to open. Nick moved to the edge and peeked around the corner. There was a semi-truck facing the exit. But Nick didn't see anyone at first glance. Once the door was all the way up, everything was quiet.

"I said hurry!" A man shouted from inside. "Your system not working got us into this. Now you'd better get me out of it. Get rid of all the evidence. I can regroup when I fire you and have a better plan!"

Nick backed away from the entrance. "Brooke, get authorities to the airport. Make sure Frost's plane doesn't leave."

"On it."

Then Nick heard the man shout again. "I don't give a shit about the girls! Bury them in the desert for all I care. Just get me out of here!"

Nick moved forward when he heard that but Allen caught him by the back of his shirt. He then pointed out to Nick the two cars parked inside the warehouse.

"I had to come here first to make sure our asses are covered," a different man spoke. Nick assumed it was Jim. Nick was still seething after hearing the way Frost just dismissed the girls' lives. When Nick heard Jim's voice it sounded like he was moving away.

"Nick!" Brooke was excited. "They were using the frequency jammers so we couldn't see them, but we can tell the car started up because headlights are hitting the building out front. They're getting away! Go, go go!"

Nick pushed Allen backward and they both ran for the front of the building. The way the road came in, the Lamborghini would have to cross in front of them to get out of the parking lot. Nick heard the whine of the high-powered engine as they rounded the corner. The headlights were facing them and Nick raised his rifle and began firing. The Lamborghini shot forward as he and Allen laid down fire. Nick was aiming for tires and Allen was shooting for the windshield.

The gunshots were loud as they reverberated off the aluminum siding of the warehouse. That's why Nick and Allen didn't hear the semi-truck start up inside the warehouse. The car continued toward them. Nick moved his aim upward and tried to put holes right through the driver's side of the windshield. It worked, the car swerved wildly to the right way off course, and slammed into the telephone pole beside the main road. They'd done it. They stopped the bastards before they even made it off the property.

At least they thought they had.

The door opened and a man slid out onto the ground. The car engine was still running. The man was lying right under a bright yellow light, and it looked to Nick to be a Mexican man. Something told him it was Hector Ramirez, but he needed to get a closer look. He took a couple steps forward when he heard the roar of another engine coming up behind them. Nick turned just in time to see the semi-truck coming fast.

It was picking up speed and headed straight for Allen.

23

Allen was focused on the man who'd fallen out of the Lamborghini, and probably the fact that it wasn't Frost, or Jim Calipari. That's why he didn't notice the massive truck driving straight for him.

"Allen! Watch out!"

Nick sprinted for Allen. As he ran he watched Allen turn and get lit up by the large headlights barreling toward him. Nick dove with all the jump he had in his legs and hit Allen at full speed. As they were on their way to the ground, Nick felt the grill of the truck bang against his boot and rip it right off his foot. That's how close he was to losing his good friend.

Nick raised up off of Allen. "You good?"

"Christ that was close."

"Where the hell are Frost and Calipari if they weren't in the car," Nick asked Allen as he helped him up.

Brooke answered for him. "They knew you were listening Nick. The Lamborghini was a distraction. They're in the truck!"

Nick hopped over to his boot. His foot was smarting, but

Saint Nick 2

it didn't feel like anything was broken. And it didn't matter to him if it was, they had a truck to catch. He whistled for his team and the reindeer floated down to the parking lot as Nick finished lacing his shoe. He and Allen got onto the sleigh and Nick commanded them forward. Now that his foot was in his boot, he felt some sharp pains. It was possible he injured it more than he thought.

The reindeer pulled forward and lifted up into the air. It didn't take long to see the truck once they got some height. The side road to the warehouse was dark. Catching the truck wouldn't be the problem. Stopping it without tipping it over or harming the girls would be the trick.

The sleigh arched back downward as the truck came into view. "I need your help now," Nick spoke to the reindeer. "I need you to land right on top of that truck. Think you can do that?"

Of course the reindeer didn't respond, but the question was actually rhetorical. He knew they could do it. There wasn't anywhere they couldn't set down the sleigh safely. They'd been doing this for a long time.

"How we going to do this without hurting the girls?" Allen asked. He was thinking the same as Nick.

The sleigh hovered right over the truck now. "Wing it," Nick said.

The sleigh touched down and immediately the truck went around a big turn. The entire sleigh shifted to the right and the reindeer scrambled to keep it on top of the truck.

Nick waved Allen off the sleigh as he held on to the rail with his off hand. "Gotta get them off of here before it falls. We're on our own, brother!"

Nick whistled twice which meant for them to go. The reindeer didn't hesitate and just like that, they were off the truck. As soon as they were outside of Nick's cloaking range, their own kicked in and they disappeared from Nick's sight. The truck hit a bump and both Nick and Allen crouched and placed both hands on the top of the truck to balance.

"Nick I have the police en route via the local FBI team down there. They should be on you in a few minutes. Call the sleigh back and get out of there. They aren't going to get away!"

"Negative. Keep the police back!" Nick shouted over the noise of the truck and the wind. "Frost said bury these girls in the desert for all he cared. He'll turn this truck over on the police if he has to. No matter what that means for the girls inside the truck!"

"All right, just be careful!"

Nick moved slowly toward the cab of the truck. The wind was blowing him back. The turns were rocking him side to side, and while the adrenaline was too high to feel the pain in his foot, he could feel something popping in his boot as he dug in with each step. Still he moved forward.

The truck didn't make the turn to get on the freeway ramp. Instead it wound around another turn, going deeper into the darkness away from the city. Frost's chilling words echoed in Nick's mind as he made it to the gap between the cab and the trailer. It was time to stop this terrible ride and bring this nightmare to a close.

Nick didn't wait for Allen. He knew his friend knew what to do. Nick jumped from the trailer to the top of the cab as soon as the truck hit a straight stretch. He didn't waste time from there, because he knew they'd heard him land. He laid out on his stomach, wormed over to the driver's side and prepared to go over. He heard Allen land behind him. He knew he would cover him by taking the cab on the passenger side.

Nick leaned over the side and paused as the truck shook

back and forth. He slipped his hand to his holster and pulled his Beretta as the wind blew in his face. He had a death grip on the seam of the truck's door. When the truck steadied, he slid off, catching the side mirror in his left hand and hitting hard with his feet on the metal step. Intense pain zinged up his right leg. Any doubt to whether or not his foot was broken had just been erased. His momentum carried him outward but he pulled himself back in by the mirror. His face went right up to the window, and that's when he found himself staring down the barrel of a shotgun.

Nick ducked just as the shotgun boomed. He was forced to let go of the mirror and as he teetered back he was just able to catch the door handle with his left hand—saving him from falling off. He raised his gun and shot right through the door about seat high. He pulled himself in toward the door, pressed the latch with his thumb and yanked the handle. The driver fell down out of the truck and nearly took Nick with him. Nick looked out in front of the truck and in the high beams, he could see it was rolling right for a drop off on the side of the road. He yanked himself up into the cab and pushed the steering wheel right. That's when he noticed Jim holding a pistol on him. Beside him sat the old man.

"Jump off or I'll shoot, Nick!" Jim shouted.

Behind Jim, Nick watched as Allen made it down to the door. He opened it and stuck his M4 to the back of Jim's head. Nick hopped up into the seat and began applying the brakes. Jim slowly put his hands up and dropped his gun.

"What's wrong, Jim?" Nick said with a smile. "Not happy to see an old pal?"

The truck slowed to a stop and Nick shut down the engine.

"Hope that money you'll never see again was fun while it lasted," Nick said.

"Go to hell."

Nick ignored him and looked over at Frost. "Sorry to ruin your comic book fantasy there Richie Rich. But you really should have known. Doesn't the good guy usually win in all those stories?"

Jack Frost didn't speak.

"Brooke, you can send in the police now. We got the truck stopped."

"What about the girls, they there?" she said.

Nick looked at Frost. "Jig is up you sick freaks. Now give me the keys to the back or your legs won't be the only things that no longer work."

Allen began fishing in the old man's pockets when he didn't move. Frost slapped his hand away and Allen hit him in the jaw so hard that Nick thought he heard it pop. Allen wasn't big on congeniality.

Allen produced the keys and tossed them to Nick. "About to find out, Brooke. Your old boyfriend and his grandpappy aren't saying much."

"Ha. Ha," Brooke said. "Police are just a couple minutes away. Want me to send the reindeer down so you can avoid the confrontation?"

"Please do."

"I'll be watching when you get in the back. I hope they aren't hurt."

Nick slid out of the truck but looked back in at Jim and Jack. "You'd better pray they're okay back there."

He hopped down and walked toward the back. His stomach had a lump in it. He was more worried about these girls than he wanted to be. He placed the key in the padlock, tossed it to the ground and popped the latch. As he opened the door, he noticed there was no light inside, and the night just outside was no help. He pulled the key fob and tapped the light at the top of it. The light was small, but it was strong. The trailer lit up in a white light and several large boxes came into view.

His heart sank.

"Nick, where are they?" There was panic in Brooke's voice.

Just as he was about to answer, there was a sliding noise at the left side of the trailer just beyond the boxes. Nick waited patiently. He took a chance and didn't reach for his gun. He didn't want the already traumatized girls to suffer any more. Even if it meant getting hurt if it wasn't them who was inside the trailer.

Finally, he saw a tuft of hair poke out from behind the box.

"Say something Nick. If it's them, you need to be soft with them. Encourage them out."

Nick swallowed hard as he thought about what to say. He was so far outside his comfort zone that he was sweating.

"Nick?" Brooke urged.

"It—it's okay. I'm not going to hurt you. You can come out."

He heard more rustling.

"I'm here to get you out of this mess."

Then the first face appeared. Nick would never be able to describe what he felt then, even if he wanted to. It was like nothing he'd ever experienced. Over on his right another face appeared. He heard Brooke gasp in his ear and the reality of the moment almost choked him up. He'd managed to keep these girls from suffering a horrible fate.

"It's them, Nick. Oh my god. It's them."

Three more faces appeared in the strange light inside

the trailer. They moved the boxes in front of them and slowly started his way.

"It's okay. You're safe n—"

Nick didn't finish his word. He was too emotional. There in the middle of the truck came one last little girl. As she walked toward him her blonde hair came into view.

"It's her..." Brooke's words broke due to emotion.

It was her. Madison's little sister. He was going to be able to fulfill his first real Christmas wish for Madison and bring her sister back to her. Tears welled in his eyes. He shook it off when the girls made it to him and he let them all fall into his arms.

Nick was never much on kids. Never cared for the sentiment of Christmas either. He was a hardass Army Ranger. But there in the back of that trailer, he changed forever.

All his life his mother tried to tell him there was magic in Christmas, but he never believed her. But tonight he knew his mom was looking down on him and his Christmas miracle, and Nick was the happiest he'd ever been.

24

Nick sat back in his chair and watched as Madison braided her sister's hair. As long as he lived, Nick would never forget the look on Madison's face when her sister hopped down out of the sleigh. Brooke came over and sat on Nick's lap. He took a sip of Colonel E.H. Taylor Barrel Proof bourbon as he squeezed his wife with his free arm. He needed the extra strong bourbon to help with the pain in his foot. Brooke urged him to get it looked at, but Nick told her it could wait.

Over in the corner, Allen was putting together a doll house for their new guests to play with. Ms. Claus had come over with cookies and some dolls for the girls as well. Nick could tell they were enjoying themselves.

"What do you think, Santa?" Brooke leaned over and gave him a kiss on the cheek. "After we deliver the presents tonight, you think you might want to make one of your own?" She nodded toward the girls.

Nick scrunched his face and gave her a sideways look. "I'm drinkin' barrel strength bourbon here, so I think your words are coming in fuzzy."

"No. I see the way you look at them. You'd be a great dad."

"There's something I never thought I'd hear. And the answer is no. I don't want one of my own. One step at a time. Lions don't forget the jungle just 'cause you put them in a zoo."

Brooke laughed. Her smile was as bright as the golden star atop the tree in the corner.

"But I wouldn't mind practicing, that's for sure," he said with a wink.

Brooke slapped him on the a chest and turned to watch the girls. Nick took another sip. He couldn't help but think about what Jim Calipari and Jack Frost were doing at that moment. He knew they were in jail, he just wondered how miserable they were. Neither one of them had a thing to say. They would soon though. When a former higher-up in the FBI and an oil tycoon come together for a human trafficking ring, a lot of media time will be spent covering that.

Madison and her sister came over and handed Nick a card.

"What's this?" He sat down his bourbon and opened the card.

"We figured Santa is always giving presents, so why not let you get one too?"

Nick smiled as he opened it. It was a cute little drawing of a rainbow behind a picture of Santa holding the hands of two little girls. "I love it." Nick said. And he really did.

"Santa?" Madison's little sister said.

"Yes darling?"

"Can you really deliver presents to all the boys and girls on earth in just *one* night?"

"Well, what do you think?"

Saint Nick 2

The sparkle in her blue eyes twinkled as she smiled. "I believe."

"Yeah? You sure?"

She nodded. "I'm sure."

"All right. In that case, since you really believe, I have a surprise for you."

The two girls smiled at each other.

"Both of you get your coats. You're coming with us."

The girls jumped up and down and Brooke hopped up to go and help them get ready. She looked back over her shoulder and gave Nick a baby making smile if he'd ever seen one. If he would have known being nice to kids was the way to a woman's bed, he might have tried to be jollier a long time ago.

"You coming, Al?" Nick got up from his chair.

"Nah, I'll leave this one for you guys," he said. "Besides, we're hanging stockings next."

Nick smiled and gave him a nod. Then he reached down and grabbed the bottle of bourbon. Since he was keeping the tradition of delivering present's just like Santa always had, he was going to keep the tradition of drinking bourbon while he did it. Just like Nick Campos would do. You can't lose yourself when change comes along. You just have to adjust, and be the best you, you can be. Ironically the best him had a bum wheel at the moment, but he managed to limp over to everyone.

As he looked at all the smiling faces in the room, there was no doubt he'd done his best this year. He supposed the real Santa would have been proud of him. A sentiment he didn't mind having a drink to. Or maybe a few drinks.

Merry Christmas to me.

The Alexander King Series
by
Bradley Wright

TAP TO ORDER TODAY!

The CIA keeps a lot of secrets.
None more deadly than him.

The Secret Weapon Sample Chapter

South of London, UK

Alexander King took a moment to steady his breathing. He'd waited a long time to kill the man who was less than a mile away from him now, but he couldn't let the anticipation affect his performance. Tonight, like every other night in his line of work, there was no room for error.

He slowed the rental car as he made a right turn off the A21 motorway onto Bewlbridge Lane. The hour long drive from London had been quiet. By eight o'clock in the evening most had settled in after a long day of work. However, King's workday had only just begun. He glanced up through the windshield at the colorful sky—an orange glow across the entire expanse hovering below a fiery layer of red. Those colors were the daylight fading, and long shadows began to throw their cast. Which was perfect, because for the last year those shadows were where he'd done nearly all of his work.

Though his flat was in the Soho neighborhood of central London, King had no need for a map to get where he was going. This was the thirty-third day in a row he'd made this particular drive. Long enough to watch hints of spring begin to blossom in the countryside southeast of the city. Every time he traveled this far into the country, a longing for where he grew up tugged at him. As he took in the rolling hills that reminded him of Lexington, he would have to blink away the running Thoroughbreds he knew weren't actually there. Kentucky—once a place he could always come back to after the wars he'd fought for his country—now seemed a place that only existed in his dreams.

King turned left and steered the car toward a small boat dock that served as an entryway into the Bewl Water reservoir. In all of his previous thirty-two trips, this was only the second time he'd made it to the docks. When you are someone who never wants to be noticed, you never keep the same pattern. Even when you *know* no one is watching. It was the same reason the car he'd driven tonight was also the thirty-third different vehicle or mode of transportation he'd taken to get there.

One can never be too careful.

King turned left off the main road and slowed to a stop. The small parking lot's streetlamps popped on overhead as he exited the vehicle. Cool air rushed him, carrying with it first the scent of mildewed wood, finishing with the sweet smell of English bluebells that carpeted the nearby fields. He could hear the boats rocking a few feet away, but nothing else.

More importantly, he could hear *no one* else.

He glanced down at his watch. Just about twenty minutes now.

He stepped from the pavement onto the wooden dock, counted four boats down on his left, and stopped when he came to the small green fishing boat. It had a large blue tackle box in the front, just like Sam had told him it would. Not that he'd doubted her. She was almost never wrong.

King stepped down into the boat, and it wobbled beneath him. His six-foot-three-inch, two-hundred-fifteen-pound frame sank the bottom a few inches. Though it had been almost five years since his last mission with the Navy SEALs, he'd never stopped the daily workouts that had become second nature. He was all muscle, but it was lean muscle. He was strong as a bull, just not so much that it took away from his agility. The things he did for a living required a lot of stealth, and a squad leader once told him, "A bull of a man never snuck up on anyone." The last few years of vigilante work and subsequent missions with the CIA had taught him as much to be true.

He untied the damp rope from the metal cleat attached to the dock and pushed back. As soon as he cleared the boats on both sides of him, he reached back and yanked the starter on the outboard motor, then grabbed the steering handle. The small engine barely roared to life, but the power of the boat was not his concern. He turned right once he cleared the dock and started down the lake. He didn't have far to go, but because he was anxious to get his hands on his target, the short ride seemed to take forever.

The light above him had been swallowed by the night, the glow of the rising moon behind him now his only guide. He took out the small set of keys left for him at a drop back in London, then scooted forward on the bench seat and opened the large tackle box. He raised the top shelf, reached in, and wrapped his fingers around the Glock 19 handgun waiting for him. It had been fitted with a suppressor can. A gift from the clandestine gods. Sam had also left him a Chris Reeve Sebenza 21 frame lock knife. Just in case a gun didn't make sense. That went in the pocket of his black tactical pants—the kind that looked civilian without losing efficiency. The last of the treats in the bottom of the box was a burner phone. He picked it up and dialed the number he'd memorized earlier.

"I see there were no problems with the drop," Sam answered, her British accent thick. He hadn't realized he was so on edge until he heard the sound of her voice, then felt the tension fall from his shoulders.

"Everything else in line?"

Normally he would have had a sarcastic line ready to throw at her, maybe something to rib her about a past failure. But not tonight.

"All I know is that no one has come or gone from the estate in the last twenty-four hours. The rest is up to you," she said.

"I'll check in when it's over."

King went to close the flip phone when he heard her voice.

"Listen, X," Sam said. X was the moniker Sam had chosen for him when she could no longer say his name in open communication. "I realize this is old hat for you. But this is the first of your targets in a long time that is personal. Just make sure you—"

"Sam," he interrupted. He could see his jumping-off point just up ahead. "I kill people who threaten my country's way of life . . . they're all personal."

He shut the phone and shoved it back into his pocket. He felt down beside his right foot, along the inside wall of the boat. His hand found the wooden handle of a single paddle. He pulled the oar into his lap and reached back to shut down the motor. The boat coasted forward, and he laid the paddle in the water at an angle that would steer him toward the shore.

Though he didn't want to think about it, he knew Sam was right. This one was more personal. This wasn't an assignment handed down from CIA Director Mary Hartsfield, the only other person on the planet who knew he was alive. This was something he and Sam had never stopped working on by themselves since the day King was forced to disappear in order to keep everyone he loved safe. He couldn't think about how close they all were to dying last year, and he couldn't focus on the fact that the man in the house just down the lake was one of the last people living who was responsible for putting everyone he loved in danger. To Sam's point, it needed to be about the kill. Not about *whom* he was killing.

The nose of the boat slid to a stop on a flat part of the bank. There was a thick wall of trees between him and the house he'd been watching for more than a month. Being so close spiked his heart rate. He let the sick feeling of unused adrenaline wash through his system as he stepped out of the boat and took a deep breath.

Though King never enjoyed taking another human's life, he'd be lying to himself if he said he wasn't looking forward to finally ending the man responsible for the death of so many innocent people. The man responsible for putting King's own loved ones in danger.

Andonios Maragos was a terrorist on the wanted list of every government agency in the world. Last year his money had funded the most terrifying attack on the White House in US history. King knew there were other people closer to the terrorist group, which Maragos was involved with, who were actually pulling the strings, but he didn't know who they were yet, and he had to start somewhere. The money was as good a place as any. And because bureaucracy had failed to pin this guilty man to any of his crimes, it was up to King to make him pay.

King wasn't sure if killing a monster like Maragos was playing God or playing the devil, but he also didn't care. Either way, the man was going to get what was coming to him.

And there was no one better suited for the work of giving Maragos what he deserved than Alexander King.

As he stepped into the shadows of the trees, King had never been more ready to do his job.

The Alexander King Series
by
Bradley Wright

TAP TO ORDER TODAY!

The CIA keeps a lot of secrets.
None more deadly than him.

ACKNOWLEDGMENTS

First and foremost, I want to thank you, the reader. I love what I do, and no matter how many people help me along the way, none of it would be possible if you weren't turning the pages.

To my family and friends. Thank you for always being there with mountains of support. You all make it easy to dream, and those dreams are what make it into these books. Without you, no fun would be had, much less novels be written.

To my advanced reader team. You continue to help make everything I do better. You all have become friends, and I thank you for catching those last few sneaky typos, and always letting me know when something isn't good enough. Alexander appreciates you, and so do I.

About the Author

Bradley Wright is the international bestselling author of action-thrillers. The Secret Weapon is his tenth novel. Bradley lives with his family in Lexington, Kentucky. He has always been a fan of great stories, whether it be a song, a movie, a novel, or a binge-worthy television series. Bradley loves interacting with readers on Facebook, Twitter, and via email.

Join the online family:
www.bradleywrightauthor.com
info@bradleywrightauthor.com

Made in the USA
Coppell, TX
24 January 2023